NIAGARA

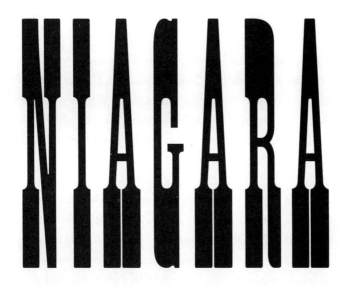

NIAGARA

A NOVEL BY RICHARD WATSON

COFFEE HOUSE PRESS :: MINNEAPOLIS :: 1993

Art by Allan Servoss.

The publishers thank the following funders for assistance which helped make this book possible: the Bush Foundation; Cowles Media/Star Tribune; the Andrew W. Mellon Foundation; the Minnesota State Arts Board; the Dayton Hudson Foundation; General Mills Foundation; the Lila Wallace Reader's Digest Fund; and the National Endowment for the Arts, a federal agency.

Coffee House Press books are available to the trade through our primary distributor, Consortium Book Sales & Distribution. Our books are also available through all major library distributors and jobbers, and through most small press distributors, including Bookpeople, Bookslinger, Inland, and Small Press Distribution. For personal orders, catalogs or other information, write to:
Coffee House Press
27 North Fourth Street, Suite 400, Minneapolis, MN 55401

LIBRARY OF CONGRESS CIP DATA

Watson, Richard, 1931-
    Niagara : a novel / by Richard Watson.
      p. com.
    ISBN 1-56689-006-3 : $19.95
     1. Man-woman relationships–New York (State)–Niagara Falls–Fiction.
   2. Stunt men and women–New York (State)–Niagara Falls–Fiction. I. Title.
PS3573.A8576N53   1993
813´.54–dc20   93-16592
                         CIP

1

ON THE WIRE

To be on the wire is life;
the rest is waiting.

— KARL WALLENDA

IGH ABOVE THE GROUND, THE WIRE. HERE is how you walk the wire. Keep your body straight but push your head forward from the chin. Keep your knees slightly bent. The pole is held on your chest by a harness, and by your two hands. The pole rests on the palms of your hands and against your thumbs. You reach around and loop your fingers over it. Do not squeeze. Hold it lightly, but firmly. The pole is twenty-four feet long and weighs forty-eight pounds. It makes your back ache. It is your life.

The wire is—or was then—four seven-eighth-inch hemp ropes wrapped tightly around a fifth to make a solid rope one and seven-eighths inches in diameter. It sags as it stretches from anchor to anchor. Every thirty feet it is guyed by two one-inch ropes, one from either side angling down and away. This is because the wire is meant to be tight. Solid. There is such a thing as slack wire walking. It is done on short ropes, by pretty little girls in petticoats, spinning parasols. The long wire is a different thing. It is rigid, serious, a man's business.

You take up the pole, jut your chin forward, look straight out over the wire and relax. Tension kills. On the other hand, tension is the essence of the wire. It is like a bowstring. Stretched, striving for release. If all the guy lines went at once, you would shoot off like an arrow in the blue.

Stretch out one foot, rest it on the wire. Press down. Feel the give? Shift your weight to the wire, back to the platform, to the wire. There is a rhythm. Your body knows when. Your back leg comes forward on its own, and you are on the wire.

Exaltation!

A shiver shoots from the base of your spine, up and out through your arms, already sweetly aware of the ache that will come before you are across.

But look! You are walking. Walking the wire. Each foot comes forward and is placed in front of the other. Short steps. Thirty steps for thirty feet.

Another world!

Yes, you see them. Those pygmies on the ground down below, and up ahead, those jackasses—local dignitaries who claim special privileges and come up on the roof with you to make things harder. You look down, of course you do. You know what is below.

But the wire is straight. You train your eyes ahead, along that line. You do not look to the side and you do not look at your feet. Your feet have eyes of their own; they see the wire.

You move along, a slowly measured step. You adjust to the heartbeat of the wire.

... For the wire lives. It has a pulse. As you walk the bounce begins. Every step increases the height of the sine waves undulating through the wire. So pause, wait, press your foot down just before the peak of the wire's rise. Introduce a second vibration to interact with and damp down the first. Then another. And another. The curves intersect, so that by the time you reach the other side there are a hundred separate pulses racing through the wire, holding one another down, keeping the wire from turning into a bucking bronco that would throw you off.

There is more. The wind. You lean into it and hope it does not suddenly stop, or change. You *always* lean with reservations. You never give yourself over to the wind. You lean just far enough and hold yourself there. You do not lean *on* the wind, you lean against it. Then if it stops, you do not tumble over. You have been *holding* yourself at the proper angle, not using the wind for support. When the wind stops, you merely move your body back. When the wind changes, you adjust to the proper angle and direction.

There is more. When walking between buildings, watch for little whirlwinds that spiral out when gusts of wind hit the buildings, split, and circle to play with you out there on the wire. And when the wire is attached to two tall buildings, there *is* a sway. The buildings themselves rock back and forth in the wind. The wire swings back and forth with them. Watch it. Feel it.

Up and down with the pulse, back and forth with the sway. It is subtle, but you must be with it, the breathing line along which you walk.

Now you have it!

That thrilling shiver again. Something happens on the wire. It is not that time does not exist there. But it is another time. It is not earth time. It is out-of-time. It is forever time, and yet you are across and it was no time.

If you like, in the middle of the wire, you can unhook your pole, balance it carefully on the wire, and stand on your head!

Sometimes I take a chair, balance it on two legs, sit down, and drink a bottle of wine!

This is how you walk the wire . . .

When I was a little boy in a tiny village in Provence, oh, six or seven years old, I ran away with a small traveling circus. It was as simple as that. I do not really know why I did it. I know that I was excited and terrified by the mangy lion (later I found she was toothless and she became my friend), and I had thrilled to the applause when I was the one—did I volunteer or was I pushed?—who went into the ring to have tricks played on him by the clown.

You know, I do not remember how many brothers and sisters I had! I used to say their names over at night—I was homesick!—but I have even forgotten most of their names now. But we were not miserable and starving. Oh, no! Papa had a farm and Mama made cheese. We had a jolly good time. I did not run away from home because I was unhappy. Far from it! I went with the circus in a surge of happiness.

There was a little circus girl. She was older than me. Nine years old, eleven? I never knew. She did tricks on the stationary trapeze. She stood on a teeter-totter and was flipped up to stand on her mama's shoulders who stood in turn on her papa's. They laughed and told me I could sleep with her, that I would have to, for their caravan was small and there was no other place.

Because of the little girl? No. Come on. I was only six or seven years old. I was a pretty little boy. I was brave. I was strong. They needed a little boy. To stick his head in the lion's mouth! To flip in the opposite direction on to *his* "mama's" shoulders! To fly from one trapeze to another!

"You must start young," they told me. Already I was almost too old to begin. It would be my career. It was an old and honored profession.

"I'll ask Papa!" I shouted.

Their faces grew round and empty. They turned away. "As you wish," they said.

I understood. They told me what time they would leave. It would be after they had taken down the equipment, in the middle of the night.

Yes, I *do* remember how I felt. Like it was yesterday. I was sad already, to leave Papa and Mama, my little dog, Milou, my brothers and sisters, my home. But I was also full of anxiety that the circus would leave without me. I told my little brother who slept with me, and he helped me keep awake. He did not seem surprised. He *cried,* but he understood. His big brother—his protector, his idol, his friend—was now going to seek his fortune, to make his way in the world, to find his métier.

They bundled me quickly into a loft shelf in the corner of the caravan, with the little girl. She complained, but went right back to sleep.

The caravan was pulled by two zebras!

When I awoke the next morning we were far from the village and the little girl was tickling me. I did not return for ten years. Papa was dead. Mama cried. My brothers and sisters and I, we did not know one another. We were too different, now.

But they were proud of me and the villagers approached me shyly. "Do you remember me?"

"Yes, yes," I would say, whether I did or not, and mostly I did not. No matter. After the show we drank wine together. But not too much. And not too late. They had to work the next day. The circus had to get on to a bigger town.

Now I am fifty—in my prime!—and have never again returned "home."

I have to laugh. I was a grown man before it occurred to me to wonder what had happened to their previous little boy. By then, there was no one who could tell me. They must have had one. All the acts had a place for a little boy—balanced against the little girl. I was thrown—and I mean *thrown*—right into the ring.

It was hard work, very hard work for a little boy. But did I know the difference? Of course not. And there was no time to have regrets.

Hauviette—that was the little girl's name—was my friend and protector. She taught me to read. The clown taught me arithmetic, all games, entirely games. I marvel at it now. When later I had to do some calculus, I found I knew the principles! He must have been a genius. Yet he was a clown.

My new "mama" taught me to write. She was impatient, much more severe than my true Mama. She cracked a whip over me. I mean it! A real whip, the same one she used with the lion!

"The world thinks we are illiterate gypsies and vagabonds," she would say. "The world is wrong!" She taught us manners, too. So many things.

Hauviette and I loved to read, and we were very good at stealing books.

Once, while Hauviette was talking up the owner of a tiny bookshop and I was in a quandary because I had slipped one too many of Jules Verne's books under my sweater, I looked up to see that he saw what I was doing. He was looking at me in the oddest way. I froze, but then felt that it was all right. I leaned over and, as best I could, made my way out the door, trying not to show more hard corners through my sweater than I absolutely had to. Hauviette stopped her chatter in mid-sentence, her smile vanished, and white-faced she followed me.

Oh, it was a topic of conversation for many a night thereafter! Nothing like that had ever happened to us before. Nor again. Several times we were caught and thrown out with boxed ears. But this . . .

Again—I seem prone to late illuminations—it came to me only years later. The bookseller had on his face a look of compassion.

I left the circus almost the same way I left home. But not before Hauviette taught me a lot more than how to read. I should say! We always slept together. Her mama had taught her what to do about *that*, too! So I never had problems of adolescence! I never knew what it was, not to have a woman. I knew how to please. I was a handsome boy! I *am* a handsome man.

But here. How I left the circus. We were a small circus, and we went from one provincial town to another. During the Easter holidays we set up in Paris, where there were many tourists. Also many other circuses and acts and shows. This tribal gathering each year was one of the few times we saw our peers and got ideas from our betters.

Here is what happened when I was sixteen or seventeen. It

was a windy day. A wire was stretched across the Seine near the newly built Eiffel Tower. On the wire was Konrad the Great and his assistant. They walked out, Konrad in front with the pole, his assistant with a hand on Konrad's shoulder walking behind. They stopped. Konrad crouched and his assistant put one foot back of Konrad's knee, stepped up with his other foot to Konrad's hip, on up to Konrad's shoulders, and carefully stood up. He stretched his arms out, Konrad adjusted to his weight and gripped the pole. Then Konrad started walking across the river with his assistant standing on his shoulders.

I was not there, but was told later. They had gone no more than ten steps when suddenly one of the assistant's feet slipped off Konrad's shoulder. The poor wretch lurched away and fell headfirst into the Seine! They were not even a hundred feet above the water, but it was said the fellow took a long time going down. He never came back up.

The crowd had forgotten to watch Konrad. He had fallen to one knee on the wire, where he teetered, but a lifetime of experience was not to be wasted by the foolish fall of an incompetent. He unhooked the pole from his chest harness, balanced it on the wire, turned around, picked the pole up again and walked back in the direction from which he had come.

Konrad swore in Polish, and in Hungarian, Turkish, and Basque. He laid down his pole, spoke harshly to another assistant in one of those languages, shouldered his way through the crowd, and walked toward the Eiffel Tower, around which several little circus groups were performing. He stopped to watch our balancing act. It was the usual supple tall pole with a platform on top. The only thing that made ours better than others was that I went up with my "papa," and while he stood on the platform, I climbed to stand on his shoulders. We held out our arms and swayed back and forth. No hands.

When we came down, Konrad was there. Like a vice he gripped me by the arm and pulled me aside. About all I could understand was that some *Scheisskopf* (I knew that was German) had killed himself and Konrad needed a young man. He dragged me through the crowd. I balked, he swore, reached into his pocket for a wallet, and put a brand new ten-franc note into my hand.

I went with him.

Then he relaxed (although he scowled at anyone who got in our way). He became jovial and told me exactly what had happened. It was a mistake only an idiot could make, a dolt, a nincompoop. Konrad sighed. It was not easy to get good help these days. The shithead had simply not been good enough. A little puff of wind had unbalanced him. Now he, Konrad the Great, had a reputation to maintain. He intended to go right back *now* and do the trick.

"You've walked a wire before, haven't you?"

Well, yes, of course I had. Who had not? But only a very short distance, and only a very few times. We did not have the equipment, it was too specialized for such a small circus as ours.

"Good!" was all Konrad said.

It is not that I had no choice. When we got down near the Seine and I saw the crowds on both banks and the roar began as Konrad climbed to the top of the platform and threw up his arms, I *wanted* to go.

Konrad said, "Put your hand on my shoulder and follow me."

I did what he said.

We walked a few steps then Konrad stopped and crouched down.

"On my shoulders," he said.

I stepped on the calf of his leg, to his hip, to his shoulders. I stood up and held out my arms.

Konrad grunted. He did not have to say anything further. He could feel that our balance was perfect.

A powerful brute of a man! He huffed loudly, but it meant nothing. Still, as we neared the other side I heard him mutter in complaint.

"What?" I said, afraid I was not hearing instructions. It was all right, you understand, but I *was* slightly out of my element.

"I said I'm getting too old for this sort of thing," he snapped, and then he laughed.

I think Konrad was sixty years old then. When we reached the other side, I jumped off onto the platform without being told. I blush. I did not just jump. As we reached the platform, I did a flip off Konrad's shoulders. He did not smile, but I could see that he was pleased. After he shook hands with the mayor, he took out his wallet and pressed another ten-franc note into my hand. "Be here early tomorrow," he said, and walked off.

I was with him ten years.

Yes, I missed Hauviette, for a while.

But!

I was soon disabused of the notion that I was a star, let alone that I even knew what I was doing. First, there was only one star in Konrad's show: Konrad. Second, early the next morning after assuring himself that I could swim and instructing me on how to enter the water from a great height just in case

—feet first and arms extended above the head, and then spread out underwater as soon as possible so as not to go too deep—Konrad sent me across the wire on my own.

I was doing wonderfully, but I knew nothing. What I did not know was that Konrad was standing on the platform behind me with a foot on the wire, introducing periodically those counter-vibrations that are necessary to keep the wire calm. Then he started reinforcing one wave, and before I knew what was happening I was riding the plunging wire like a small boat in a heavy sea. As I pitched over, I caught a glimpse of him, arms crossed, watching. The *Scheisskopf!*

But it was no time to be angry at the discovery that he had set me up. I adjusted my body to the proper angle and waited a long time.

Then I hit. Water jammed up my nose and into my eyes and hurt my ears, but all was in order and there was no surprise. I fought my way to the surface and set out with a strong stroke for the shore, to kill Konrad. I ignored the boat which came out to retrieve the pole.

When I reached the bank, Konrad pulled me from the water with one hand and twirled me around with my arm stretched up. A small crowd of early risers out to watch us practice broke into applause and I automatically took a bow.

"Now shall we begin?" Konrad said, and took me right back up.

He knew I had had my fill for the day, and did not make me go on the wire again. Instead he went out—backward—and walking toward me, introduced me to the technique of controlling the wire's pulse.

"Put one foot on the wire," he commanded. "Feel!"

I was adept. I soon learned how to counter the pulse of the wire.

After that lesson, Konrad went out without the pole and, to my horror, fell off immediately. There was no water below, only the concrete pilings of the river bank. But he did not die. No, as he fell he caught the wire with both hands and hung on firmly.

Konrad the Great gave me a big wink!

Then he swung up onto the wire again. "Always," he said, standing there nonchalantly, "if you are always ready, no matter how you fall, you have time to twist and catch the wire."

So saying, he leaned over sideways like a falling tree, and at the last possible moment twisted around to grab the wire.

"Of course, the worst," he said, coming back up on the wire again, "is if you straddle," at which word his legs shot apart. He caught himself with his hands stretched down between his legs, rose to a handstand, and walked on his hands along the wire back to the platform.

"If you miss that one," he grimaced, "no more fucky-fucky."

Konrad set up a short wire for me to practice falls in the courtyard of the hotel (no more caravans, from here on I lived in style, and traveled only to the largest cities of Europe, by train). It was twenty feet up, "to make it interesting."

"Never practice at a low height where it doesn't matter," he said. "From the very beginning, when you are on the wire, it *always* matters."

Nor did he ever use a net. Once he showed me how to catch. He stood below and told me to fall feet first, and he caught me around my legs to let me slide down the length of his body to slow the fall. I landed standing up.

"What about when I'm standing on your shoulders?"

He frowned. "Then we don't fall," he said.

Nevertheless, he beckoned to a couple of assistants, and climbed up the ladder to the practice wire.

"If you do not *launch* yourself, as that idiot did, when? Last year? Last month? Only yesterday? If you do not *launch* yourself out away as you fall, you will always drop within reach of the wire. You must hold on very tight, for there will be a shock. Always be ready for that shock. Your arms can take it if you are ready."

He picked up a pole. "Ready?"

I could not even nod. We went out onto the wire and I climbed up on his shoulders. He paused just a moment, and then he dropped out from under me. His pole went to the right and he grabbed the wire a body's length behind where I would fall straight down. I dropped and grabbed the wire.

Oh, it did wrench my shoulders! But I held, and well that I did, because it was obvious that the assistants were more concerned with avoiding being hit by the falling pole than with catching me. The falling Pole? They would certainly have caught Konrad, who would kill them if they did not. But me?

"You're not as smart as I thought you were," Konrad said, swinging back up onto the wire. He walked to the platform and got another pole. "Now get on my shoulders again."

I did it trembling. Enough was enough.

"Now *think* with your little pea brain," Konrad said. "Wouldn't it be more graceful if you landed on your feet on the wire? Try it!"

I could feel Konrad's body braced. I was sure I could do it. But I knew I had to look out for myself. Nobody was going to catch me. I stepped lightly off his shoulders and dropped into a standing position on the wire, bounced and landed again, on my feet.

"Again."

I did it. I knew what was coming, but not that day. Nevertheless, within a week I was doing a flip off Konrad's shoulders and landing on the wire. He got me to try it the first time only by positioning four assistants below and swearing that he would kill them if they did not catch me. I did not fall off the wire. The first time, I admit, I fell over and went down on my chest on the wire right after I hit. But it was only because I had been afraid. A single flip to the wire from Konrad's shoulders? A mere child could do that, and fry an egg on the way down!

Konrad was not particularly eager to teach me his own routine, but he did not forbid me to imitate. I watched him, and then practiced. I *never* fell except when I knew I was going to. I *always* caught the wire, swung back up, and tried again. I turned somersaults, stood on my head, sat on a chair, pushed a wheelbarrow. Just trying it out.

Sometimes Konrad could not resist. *"Nyet!"* he would bark, having just happened to walk by, and he would swarm up the ladder and show me how it was done.

We both knew I would soon be better than he was with the tricks. Except I did not have sixty years behind me of doing them. Konrad was sarcastic and mean, but sometimes when you expected the worst, he would laugh at himself. I was soon doing standing flips on the wire, front and back. With the bounce in the wire I was sure I could do a double, but I hesitated to try it. I could have rigged a safety rope tied to my waist, extended to a pulley up above, with a man below holding the other end if I missed, the way all the fliers learn their tricks, but Konrad would have frowned. It would not have been being serious on the wire. Or perhaps he would not have. Was he harder on me than he had been on himself?

I was thinking about trying it, the double, when he shouted up. "Double?"

I nodded.

"I'll show you," he said, coming up the ladder.

I was speechless. Konrad was a big man. I had never seen him do more than a somersault, not even on the ground.

He waved me off and went out on the wire and started bouncing up and down. "Hup!" he shouted and jumped up, stretched out his arms and legs, and landed flat on his stomach on the wire. He bounced up, his body horizontal to the ground, and revolved around 360 degrees like a plate on a stick, came down flat on his stomach on the wire again, and then bounced up to land standing on his feet. He took a handkerchief from his back pocket and theatrically mopped his brow.

"That's one," he said, "but I'm getting old. I don't think I can still do a double." Then he laughed without humor.

When he came back to the platform, he looked deep into my eyes and patted me on the shoulder. "Don't push it just yet," he said, and climbed down.

I climbed down after him. We knew I could do it. Maybe I was not ready yet, maybe I *was* pushing too hard, but we knew who I was pushing. There was no hurry.

Konrad was a man of sixty. He had been on the wire since he was born . . . before, really, as his mother continued her slack-wire act into her seventh month. His father took him out on the high wire in a special sling before he was a month old. As a tot, he rode the shoulders of his parents and his uncles and aunts in a very famous act.

It was a wonderful act, a marvelous family. The Great Kulezas: three generations on the wire. Not the long wire Konrad and I walked. No, the high wire, usually as part of a big circus, near the top of the tent or hippodrome. They walked on their hands, stood on their heads, sat on tiers of chairs.

Their big act was the human pyramid. Konrad's father and one of his uncles walked with a rod stretched on shoulder harnesses between them, another uncle and a brother followed also with a rod. Konrad and a cousin stood on the two rods, with a third rod stretched from shoulder harnesses between them. On that top rod, Konrad's mother stood slim and tall.

They walked across the tight wire, never a great distance, forty feet at most. Then they walked back, backward. In the middle they might stop for Konrad's mother to stand on her head and turn a somersault.

It was a famous family and it was a famous fall. Nobody made a mistake. The Kulezas never made a mistake on the wire. These things happen. One of the lower rods broke, the one stretched between Konrad's father and his uncle. It should not have, but it did. Konrad's mother fell to her death. Konrad's father caught the wire and then was pulled off when he tried to catch his brother, and they both fell, the brother breaking a leg and Konrad's father his back. For a few years thereafter he was seen with the troupe, laid out on a wheeled stretcher, shouting crotchety instructions. Then they put him away or he died, I never knew.

The others caught the wire, including Konrad, trained from babyhood, who had landed on it and hung on. They pulled themselves up and walked to a platform and climbed down.

The show went on, of course it did. Even the same stunt. Konrad was seventeen or so at the time. It was a big family and they all knew this sort of thing happened. I am sure Konrad mourned his parents. He never said anything about it to me, I learned all this from others.

When Konrad got older and had more say, he began putting up longer wires. He complained about the crowded conditions on the high wire, of claustrophobia under the tent ceiling, of the bondage of always having to work so precisely and in such close interdependence with others.

Before Konrad had established the long-wire act as part of the show, a wire collapsed under him. Not all the way, and he was fortunate that he was not killed. He scooted to a sagging guy wire and slid down.

That might have been the end of it except that he had hardly reached the ground before a young man with wild eyes accosted him.

"Andreas Hartle, licensed engineer," the young man said, and immediately started telling Konrad what had gone wrong. Hartle was a German trained to build bridges. Now he saw in front of him a very long bridge with but a single strand of right-of-way. Konrad was infected by Hartle's enthusiasm, and together they began to build longer and longer "bridges." Hartle was fascinated with the challenge of setting up the wire in new locations, from every kind of building and platform in city after city. It is not usual for performers to be close friends with technicians, but Konrad and Hartle became friends.

Within a year Konrad left the family to go on his own as:

Not to forget his partner Andreas Hartle, bridge builder *extraordinaire.*

Then one day after they had been together for several years, Hartle came to Konrad to say good-bye.

"But why?"

Hartle was going to be married. Konrad was flabbergasted. The women came to Konrad, but he always made sure that Hartle got his share. Was that not enough? Or why not bring her along? After all, Konrad had grown up on the road. They could have children. It would be no problem.

Hartle smiled and shook his head. Neither of them said anything about putting up the wire. Konrad had learned. He knew as much now as Hartle. They said good-bye.

I wonder if Konrad was ever my friend? I think so. But at least I had found my master and my métier. You may think ten years was a long apprenticeship. I never thought about it. But it was always just in the back of my mind that Konrad could not walk the wire forever. He was growing old. I would inherit the act and be on my own before I was thirty as:

GRAVELET THE GREAT!

Hauviette cried when I told her I was leaving. But my circus mama and papa were proud. The next day they shut down their show at noon—the best time of day—and rushed over to watch me perform. There I was, as though I had done it forever, a hand lightly on Konrad's shoulder as we walked out on the wire.

Three steps to stand on his shoulders, a "Hup!" and a "Ho!" my arms outspread, and Konrad walking. The lay-out flip off his shoulders to the platform at the end.

But—*Mon Dieu!*—this second time, I was terrified!

I now knew that Konrad had to tame the wire with dozens of gentle nudges out of phase with dozens of different vibrations. Otherwise, we would be pitched off. I really did not want to fall again. I also knew now—for many people had told me—that the river was deep enough only at the exact point where Konrad had dumped me in. Otherwise, I would have been crushed on the bottom, driven deep into the mud—as perhaps my predecessor had been—dead and buried in one blow.

That did not bother me. Konrad knew what he was about. In this business—standing on poles, swinging on trapezes, walking wires—there are always slender envelopes inside which you are safe. We stay within those margins. They are invisible to spectators. Konrad had flipped me off the wire that morning precisely at the only safe place.

Now we could not fall. Did I say that in this business what you do is *always* serious?

We started out over the street, then the pilings on the bank, then the mostly shallow river, and then pilings on the other bank, and another street. I must have been crazy to do a flip off Konrad's shoulders to the platform just before he stepped off the wire that first time. Did I have to do it again? Yes, that second time I could feel his body preparing for it. The first time he took it because he was always ready for *anything,* but now—now he expected it and I had to do it.

Actually, it was nothing. I make too much of it. We play, you know, to the crowd.

I suppose you want to know about the women. No, that is not the right tone. I do not mean to be condescending, I do not want to belittle other men's experience. It is inevitable that I have had more women than the ordinary man. I am a tall and handsome fellow—would you believe? I grew and grew. It must have been the exercise. Nearly six feet tall, 165 pounds, all muscle, I towered over most men. And strong! I tell you!

Hauviette kept me from the girls as much as she could. When I got away she sighed and groaned. She warned me about diseases. She preached the virtues of soap and of "French letters" (which I never used). When I roamed, she inspected me carefully afterwards and held me off until she was sure I had not caught a disease.

The dear thing! She was protecting herself. One day she wished to have a baby.

Perhaps our circus mama and papa really were her true parents. Anyway, she would not leave them, although I begged her to. They could carry on until they found a replacement for me, but if she too left, they would have had a very hard time. So she stayed with them. (Did she ever have a baby? I do not know, I lost track.)

Hauviette went back to her trapeze, and I went on to other girls!

A man like me has no trouble getting women. If anything, there is a problem of deciding which. You soon learn to spot the crazy ones, the "hysterics." And after you have broken the hearts of a few young girls, if you have any compassion, you do not have the stomach for more of that, sweet as they are, dear things. Not the frightened ones, not the bawds, not the brazen or the bizarre. Not women on the rebound, not women punishing their husbands, not women trying to make their boyfriends jealous, not celebrity fuckers, not women seeking publicity.

No whores.

No. Perhaps it is hard to believe, but I always go for the mousy ones. I do not mean that they look like mice! I mean the demure ones. They are not shy, but they do not push forward. Their hair is put up nicely, they smell good, and they wear modest round hats that cover their heads and come down almost over their eyes. They are well dressed, good cloth on their bosoms, stylish folds to their ankles. Perhaps a parasol. You watch the parasol, probably it twirls.

You catch her eye. She seems startled. You shrug. She looks down, and then glances up out of the corner of her eye. You smile. An enormous smile! Why do I say "you"?

Me! I smile, I inflate my chest, my body stands out of the crowd and says, "Me! Me! Me!"

She smiles wryly. (The dance proceeds.) My face takes on a look of exquisite longing. Against hope my eyes yearn. My arms rise, my hands and shoulders make the slightest of movements. It is a question.

"Will you, oh will you, please, young madam?" For *of course* she is a married woman. "Will you come to me after I walk the wire? I am a man! My life is a life of danger in defiance of death. I am vulnerable. I am simple. I live from day to day. Your quiet beauty, your charms, have devastated me. I am full of desire. *I want you!*"

I relax and spread my arms wide. I bow my head. Through the crowd she looks at me. She smiles broadly now. She drops her chin, the sign is barely perceptible. She has said, "Yes!"

I know. She sees that I know. I am ecstatic. Quietly, of course. She turns her back and makes as though to stroll off. But she looks over her shoulder. Yes, she will be there.

The best have been married for years, married in their teens to older men. Now they are thirty. They do not tell me how old they are, but I know. That is the best age. You remember I started with an older woman? Older women are always best. Thirty, forty, even fifty. Do not laugh. I know.

They are not unhappy with their plight. No Emma Bovarys here, but they have all *read* Flaubert. They are delighted and amazed when they find that I have, too. "Research," I tease them.

Usually this is not their first adventure. Whether it is or not, I do my best with every one to make her happy. Her pleasure is my own, and I know how much more is a woman's pleasure in making love than a man's. They know it, too, but their husbands are too busy or too old or too bored or they just do not care.

I know. I care. I please them if I can. Is it not my duty to make them happy, to encourage them to make other conquests to brighten their little lives? Duty! Was I not instructed by an older woman? Am I not a Frenchman? Well, then!

You want to know more about the women? So, my friend, do I!

These women often tell me about their lives, spreading their small hands on my hard muscled body, sighing with pleasure in my bed. They tell me of their daily round, and of their dreams. When I was younger, I mistook their fantasies for unfulfilled desires. They are not that at all! These women do not really wish to run away with me (a frightening thought!), or to write a novel, or to be a nurse and follow the wars. They are realistic, and even content, in their bourgeois lives. Still, there is one fantasy they can make real. They can go to bed with me! No one will know. Or at least those who do—sometimes their own husbands—pretend not to. It is exciting and no one is hurt.

Is it really like that? I really do not know. Most of them put up a good front. Of course, sometimes they cry.

"Why your tears, little one?"

"Never mind," she says, dabbing at her eyes with a hanky. "It's because I'm silly, it's because you make me happy."

Sometimes I believe what they say.

Enough of girls for now. After Hauviette I never had a steady woman. We traveled too much, there was no woman in our entourage. This was Konrad's way. He said women on the wire always cause trouble.

We had plenty of applicants. For the wire as well as for our beds! Sometimes we would take one across. Konrad would carry her on his back. I preferred the wheelbarrow. We took only the innocents. Real lady wire walkers need not apply.

No, I am not Don Juan, but I wonder if I have not had as many women! (I see I am not ready to leave the subject after all.) What was it Don Juan had: 1,003? We know—Don Juan and I—how to please a woman in bed. I wonder if we know anything else about women? Surely we do, for they confide so much to us. Yes, but we do not always listen. Alas, sometimes when we listen, we do not hear. Yet they tell and tell.

It would be an exaggeration to say that I have had as many women as Don Juan. I have had many women but—how shall I say it?—I did not always need a woman. For long stretches the wire was enough. I think in part, also, I did not always need a woman because, as I said, I never knew the lack.

Nor is it quite true that I never had a steady woman for any length of time. *I* did, and so did Konrad, but it always caused trouble. Eventually Konrad's woman always wanted me. I swear to God! That is the way it was. I never went after Konrad's women. They came to me!

I told them, "No!" All those things. You know how *that* goes. They took my words only as matters of form, and my refusal as a tease and challenge. I was not uncorruptible, after all, I like women as much as they like me, and Konrad picked plump bouncy lasses who were a lot of fun.

"Konrad's *good,* they would whisper and wiggle, "but he's not . . . enough . . . for me . . ."

That always got me. I was never capable of turning down a damsel in distress.

What happened to Nicole, Francine, and Coquette? I know

that at least Nicole got married and had babies. She wrote and told me.

Nicole was so dramatic. She swore that she would kill me and herself. Because I did it to a little piece of fluff? Nonsense. Nicole knew I always had women on the side, so why did she come screaming at me one day with a knife? I grabbed it from her. She ran away sobbing.

I was worried!

Then the next morning there was a hullabaloo outside my window. I got up to look. It was Nicole, in a wagon, a sturdy lad holding the reins and not looking up. Nicole was standing. She threw kisses at me with both hands and tears streamed down her face. Even so, she looked fierce and proud. Her bags were all packed in the wagon. Her country boyfriend had come to get her. That was what it had been all about. Konrad sneered at me scornfully. The fellow had been around for days and I had not even noticed!

Good-bye, Nicole.

Francine? I do not know. We were in Paris and one day she was gone. I looked as best I could, but Konrad and I had to walk the wire, take it down, and catch a train for Berlin. Paris was where she had joined me, a year and a day before. It was her city. She knew I would not have time to find her. She never wrote.

Then there was Coquette.

We should not have had steady women. I said we did not let them walk the wire. That is true. We did not give them per-mission. Coquette did not ask. She wore tights and a petticoat fringing her pert *derrière*. She bribed our assistants. One day when Konrad and I reached the other side, we heard cheers more than for us, and turned to see Coquette already on the wire.

Yes, she had made me teach her on the practice spans. I had thought it a good plan to indulge her because she was Konrad's woman and I was holding her off. Now Konrad made a move to go on the wire to monitor its pulse, but held back. Coquette did quite nicely by herself, *s'il vous plaît!*

Konrad was furious. I was amused. There was no turning back. The crowds now would demand Coquette. That night she came to my bed and stayed with me, how long, eighteen months? Konrad, for once, said not a word. He did not want competition in bed with him.

Coquette.

One day she fell. I do not know why. Konrad said one word: "Suicide." Probably he is right but it is hard to believe. She simply went to the center of the wire—it was strung from the clock tower to the hotel in Munich—out over the paved square, and she stood there a long time. Then she bent over from the waist and balanced the pole on the wire, took a few steps forward, and fell gracefully to the street. Yes, quite gracefully!

A fellow in the crowd made as though to catch her, but he got out of the way just in time. A good thing. It was too far, and there would have been two smashed bodies rather than just the one.

Konrad ordered me to go look. Before I could argue, he picked up a pole and went walking out to retrieve Coquette's, still balanced on the wire. Her pole could fall and kill someone, and then we *would* be in trouble.

I was angry that Konrad thought I should go look. I knew what it would be like. I did not have to see. I went because it was Coquette. They raised a corner of the coat someone had put over her. I looked and nodded. A cart came and took her away.

I said I did not know why. On the other hand, I was not surprised. How do I reconcile these two statements? If I was not surprised, I ought to know, had I not?

I am not, basically, an introspective man. What I mean is that what I think, I think out in the open. I do not sit quietly by myself in a corner and brood on inward thoughts. No, what I think, I say. Coquette heard me say it many times.

Coquette loved me. I loved her! But she wanted us to marry. She wanted my child! I laughed and tickled her.

"Coquette, Coquette, you silly goose. This is no life for a married man. What will the child do after his father falls to his death?"

I joke a lot about falling, of course, because it is good for business. Then, I *am* ready. Finally, I do know that if I keep walking all my life—and I see no reason not to, it is a good life—that if I continue to walk the wire, one day I will fall.

Coquette preferred to face the inevitable in the guise of Konrad.

"He's getting too old," she would say. "Look how he shakes when you climb on his back. You're getting too heavy for him. You'll both fall."

How seriously could I take this? Because the next thing she would say was that she should take my place standing on Konrad's shoulders. Better, she should ride on mine. I refused to let her try. If Konrad had seen us, he would have gone mad with rage.

There was that, her own ambition, at cross-purposes with undercurrents of fear and hope. What she meant when she said she wanted to have a baby was that we should leave the wire, settle down. We had enough money to start in some shop or business.

Of course, that was ridiculous!

Coquette knew perfectly well that I would never leave the wire. Give up a life of excitement, travel, and stardom to be a bourgeois shopkeeper? *Paterfamilias?* Me? Never!

We *had* a good life, I reassured my little Coquette. I even hinted that I knew that she had her own adventures with local swains. I did love her best of all, but she was not really worried about *that*. She understood. She had a feeling for the wire herself. After all, she was a walker.

What more did we need? We were always lifted by the wire. It was always there, always to be walked. Our blood pulsed and vibrated with the wire. We did not live an ordinary life of contented boredom, of somnolence, half alive, like the common herd. We always felt the thrill of mortality in our bones. Our lives were always serious. We were always on the wire.

What about a son? Yes, I would like to have a son! If I fell, what would the poor child do without a father, or a mother if she fell? Bah! That is drivel. Both Coquette and I knew it was a pitiful excuse. Konrad would see to him. Someone would. We did, after all, belong to one of the last guilds in Europe. Informal as it was, we took care of our own. My son, our son, would be taken care of by some "mama" and "papa" just as I was by mine. Should I fall, he would carry on. It made me proud to think so.

Alas, I was not ready to have a son. It is never too late for a man. For a woman . . . well, Coquette was older than me. I am not sure, but I think she was forty. She had been an acrobat before she came to us, had done flips from teeter-totters onto men's shoulders. Perhaps she thought her time had passed. She knew perfectly well mine had not.

I am not an introspective man, but this does not mean that I do not think, nor does it mean that I do not strive to understand.

Within six months after Coquette fell, The Great Konrad was dead. I think there is a connection between the two, but I do not know what it is. That is, a connection that would be an explanation to me of something about life. I wonder, for example, if there is any significance in the fact that the two falls were diametrically opposite in cause. Without her pole, Coquette had only the slightest hope of walking the wire to the end. She was courting death. Konrad, on the other hand, was doing what he had done a thousand, many thousand times before in his lifetime. He had every right to expect that he would do it successfully again.

I was on his back.

Yes, I *had* become too heavy for him. When he first took me on, I must have weighed no more than 125 pounds, perhaps less. Add the 48 pound pole, and Konrad was carrying nearly 175 pounds on walks of several hundred feet. Ten years later, *I* weighed close to 175 pounds. Add the pole and Konrad was carrying over 200 pounds. You do not believe it? Listen, I have seen a man walk a wire with a 48 pound pole, and on his shoulders stood a lad weighing 125 pounds and on *his* shoulders a boy weighing 90 pounds—nearly 300 pounds.

Look, I have seen the bottom men of some of the great Bulgarian teeter-totter acts, those anchor men with broad shoulders and enormous bellies and massive legs, I have seen them walk around the ring carrying on their shoulders four men stacked one on top the other, a tier five men high, 600 pounds! And that Bulgarian, he stands strong and straight, he does not stagger, he walks firmly and in great control.

On the ground, I grant you, but it can be done.

I was a little heavy for Konrad, but not *that* heavy. In his prime he could easily have . . .

I would guess that Konrad was seventy when he died. Coquette was right. We should have presented him with a fait accompli. We should simply have sent Coquette out behind him one day and that would have been that. He would have had to accept her and after that—just as when she first walked—the crowds would have demanded that he carry the pretty girl in tights and petticoat.

Coquette was gone, and Konrad continued to carry me. We walked out on the wire. Konrad crouched, I stepped on the inside of his knee, to his hip, onto his shoulders. Konrad crouched down further. This was not right. He was supposed to straighten as I stood on his shoulders.

I could feel his effort. He stood up. "My knee," he said quietly. Then his right leg collapsed.

I did what I had to do. There was plenty of time. You always have plenty of time when your heart rate leaps to 200 beats a minute. When every split-second movement is, as I have re-marked before, very serious. I saw clearly—as though time had slowed—what went wrong with Konrad.

His injured knee made his right leg useless. As he crumbled to the right, he should have let his pole go to the right. But for some reason—I suppose his instinct was that he should try to recover his balance—he tipped the pole to the left, just for an instant, then he let it go right. I stepped off his shoulders as he dropped. We were going to belly on the wire, none of this fancy stuff of falling by and catching it with your hands!

No tricks!

Konrad hit the wire with his chest, reached over with his arms, and then I hit the wire behind him. His body rose, floated over the wire, and slid back. He still had his arms out and would catch. Then the wire bounced up again, tapped Konrad lightly on the chin, he jerked back, his fingertips brushed the wire, and he drifted away, slowly, oh so slowly, back and down and away, his arms outstretched, his eyes focused on the wire.

"Wait!" I wanted to shout, but I was mute.

"Come back. There is time. We can do it again. This time you let the pole go to the right immediately. You do not lose that split second when you tried to recover your balance. Then when I come down, and the wire comes up, it just grazes your chin. It smacks into your two hands, and you *hold!* You hold as you could have held a line thrown out by a speeding locomotive. You hold as you could even if your arms were torn from their shoulder sockets. You had a grip that no man in Europe could endure. You won bets in bistros with that grip."

"Konrad! Wait! Hold on!"

But perhaps not. Maybe an elbow would have gone, too. He was too old. His knee collapsing did not kill him. His recovery was not perfect. *He made a mistake!* The consequences were serious. He always said they would be. On the wire, what one does, it is always serious.

Konrad, was he an introspective man? He was as matter-of-fact as I about the reality of danger on the wire, but he never joked about falling as I did. After my predecessor fell and after Coquette fell, he seemed not to be emotionally affected at all. Oh, he swore, but otherwise he seemed to ignore that they were dead, just gone, and he went right on with what he had to do. He went on until he was too old for the wire.

How do you know when you are too old? Well, if you wait long enough, the truth will come through the wire. You have to be honest with the wire, because the wire is always honest with you. It never lies.

I sat on the wire. We had an assistant who could come out

with a pole, but I could see he was not going to. I sidled along on my seat. Several times I got up and ran ten feet, then sat down again. I might have run all the way without a pole, probably I could have, but I did not feel like trying just then. I slid on my ass!

Yes, the show must go on. There were two more walks scheduled, and I did them. We were already diminished by Coquette. Now with Konrad gone, it was a one-man show.

(Gravelet the Great?)

It could not be denied. It was coming through. I wonder if the volume was not building up even as Konrad fell. The thunder.

Now!

I did not look for someone else. Several applied, but I had lost my stomach for working with others. And on my very first walk as solo performer I started exhibiting what I would build into an enormous repertoire. I stood on my head, I jumped backward, I pretended to fall. And now? What can I *not* do on the wire?

That, too, jackass! Just find me a woman who will comply!

Let us talk about wire walking. Not now about walking the wire, but *being* a wire walker. As a joke, I say that suddenly I rose up in the world. There is a certain status in being a circus performer—you can behave familiarly with the general public in ways not permitted to everyone. But when you become a wire walker, someone like Konrad, someone like me, you are no longer a mere circus performer. You become, I became . . .

An Artist!

The wire walker has an aura. I know what it is. Other performers have skills and techniques. Indeed, an ordinary tumbling acrobat has more skill than the usual wire walker. Not more than me, of course! I do the tumbling tricks myself!

On the wire!

The wire walker has an aura of perfection. He generates awe in all who see and know him because he is perfect in what he does. He is the embodiment of perfection on this earth, or rather, above it, on the wire, where all can see. He is perfect because otherwise he could not be. Perfection is his essential attribute. If he were not perfect, he would not exist. One lapse and he is dead.

Watching a wire walker is as close as many people will ever come to being in the presence of God!

Please do not misunderstand. I am not a humble man. But I am not crazy. I know I am not divinity incarnate. Far from it!

But I do know what Simeon Stylites was trying to say when he spent his life on his upended pole. He was striving to make a point. As I am now.

As a perfectionist, I was welcomed by others of my kind. Painters, poets, ballet dancers, bullfighters, even musicians, those tunesters who begrudge space in the Pantheon for other artists less close to the celestial spheres. Ah, but they, even they, had to admit my right. They merely capture the vibrations of God on catgut. I walk in God's heaven on the singing wire.

We artists, we understand one another. Ballerinas perhaps understand me best of all. (What women! What strength in their thighs!)

But all hold their breaths and watch as I carve like a sculptor my steely statement against the sky.

And they do, me, in paint and stone and music and poems . . . and the ballerinas in their beds!

I know the galleries, the lofts, the studios, the garrets and halls and theatres and cafés of Paris, Rome, Berlin, Buda and Pest, Amsterdam, Vienna, Prague, and Copenhagen. I have walked the wire in Moscow, Constantinople, and Petrograd. Before kings and queens and czars. I wear a frock coat with as much ease as an acrobat's tights. I deign to speak their languages with my charming French accent.

Konrad taught me how to behave. Heels together, the slight bow, Austro-Hungarian lilt in the gestures of the hand and chin, the casualness in one's clothes of an aristocrat born of the blood.

A French peasant! Bah, what do you think circus performing is? I have been an actor all my life.

I am what I am. I told you. A perfect human being. A man who is not permitted to make a mistake. Perfect within limits, you understand. Perfect on the wire. But can we not admit that some of that perfection seeps into other attributes of my being? Just a bit? In bed? Is not a woman like a wire, a trembling living thing that must be stroked and touched with delicate precision, with infinite care? One must advance by instinct along the path to bring the mounting wave of passion to its full expression. Ah, there is an art!

You come to them with your pole and you walk the wire upright and never betray the effort it costs. Either you deny your body the relief of exhaustion or you are dead. This, too, is a serious thing. If there were exhibitions in the capitals of Europe of *this* amazing skill, would I not be doubly renowned!

No, it is not all brushes with death and ballerinas. I have gone to Morocco to perform in winter, but there is a season. I like three months in the winter alone. I do well for myself. I have a villa on the Côte d'Azur near Cannes. I trim the grapes in winter. How could I have nostalgia for the farm? My peasant blood? Yet I am never home for the harvest.

I never take a woman to my villa. Well, not never. But better is to hire a saucy country maid.

I read. I stroll about. I take a glass with the farmers in the village.

I have my practice wire. I keep in shape, and try to teach the old dog new tricks.

Long before the three months are over, I admit, I get restless. It is not so far from my villa to the railroad line. The train goes from Nice down the coast to Marseilles, and then up through Provence and central France to Paris. I can be in Paris in twenty-four hours. Often I am. Sometimes I return the next day.

I wonder if the only time I am at peace is on the wire? Then I am where I am meant to be. There time does not matter. Maybe that is why sometimes I take the train to Paris and then turn around and come right back. It is like a walk on the wire!

Alas, even perfection has its drawbacks. Women sometimes accuse me of a certain coldness. There are women of such exquisite sensibility that they perceive my flawless technique itself as a lack.

I need a beauty mark! A black spot, an ugly cicatrix to set off so much more the perfect form of my cheek.

For some women, my impeccable ministrations are suspect. For them I press down to start a counter vibration, insert an epicycle to make the repeated rise more interesting as that revolution comes again and around once more.

"Ahh!" I say with this one, "I couldn't hold, I came too soon." All the more to increase the amplitude of her own release in utter pride that even one as strong as I could not hold out against her charms.

With another, I plead fatigue and beg that she ride me.

In the end it all comes to the same thing. Some women watch and know, whatever carousel you wind up for them to ride.

Did I say I was fifty? Actually, I am sixty. I was fifty when I last saw Taylor. Off and on, I have been thinking about her for ten years. It is not that I want to stop thinking about her. A serious intellectual problem of great complexity is a good thing to have for occupying one's mind. If life were simple, then where would we be?

Actually, what we did, my assistants and I, those winter months is the same thing we had always done when Konrad was alive. We worked like slaves on the equipment, the ropes, the cables, the sleeves, the buckles and hooks, the clamps and pulleys and stretchers and stakes. And do you realize how much work it is to maintain a rope a thousand feet long? Here, too, we could make no mistakes.

We do not use rope anymore. We use steel cable.

Did I say I was an artist? Yes, but that is not all. Konrad also made me, like himself, into an engineer. I even understand the mathematics of stress and counterpoise, which he never did.

You see only the outer form, but in every work of art there is an inner structure. It is frustrating. Konrad and I will go down in history as the greatest funambulists who ever lived, but few people will ever realize that we were also two of the greatest engineers of our time. Hartle solved the basic problems, but Konrad had to go on and make the bridges work. I exceeded him. The wire was still a rope when Konrad died. Some years later I started experimenting with steel cables. I built fantastic new "bridges" that Konrad never dreamed of. *All* the walkers build them my way now.

So what? It is what is up front that counts, right?

Konrad left everything to me. There was not a lot of money because he lived well and had spent it on good restaurants, good hotels, and first-class railway accommodations. And on women. He had not stinted. He had taken me right along with him, and he made sure his lesser assistants were comfortable. He never said to me in so many words, "Do not be cheap and miserly, share your good fortune with your co-workers who help make it possible." He did not have to say it, he lived it—as long as everyone understood that he was number one. He could be vicious if someone tried to step in front of him.

What he left me was all I wanted—the wherewithal to ply my trade.

But alas! Now that I was number one, no one knew it!

I went on to finish Konrad's contracted walks, but suddenly there were no new inquiries. It was as though wire walking were no longer of interest. I had no work!

What had happened was clear to see. They knew only Konrad. Never mind that anyone who knew what it was all about could see that during those last few years, Coquette and I carried him. After Konrad fell, it was as though the city councils and the public thought that there were no other walkers, and that there would never be another.

I understood. Konrad the Great was the attraction. One's grandfather had seen him walk fifty years ago. Konrad was a European institution. No matter how good, no one was soon going to take his place.

I beat my brow. Think! I was *not* going to go back to small time. I was *not* going to wait fifty years, or even ten.

Oh, that there were *two* Eiffel Towers!

The answer came to me in a carnival sideshow. There it was in a panorama of the seven wonders of the world—Niagara Falls!

I rushed to a library and looked in the encyclopedia. Yes! The distance was fine. There was surely competition for tourists between the Canadian and United States sides. My walk would unite and benefit them both.

I could speak some English, that most difficult and barbaric tongue. After all, I had been many times with Konrad to London—then to Manchester, Leeds, Dublin, Edinburgh . . .

I addressed my letter to THE MAYOR, NIAGARA FALLS, UNITED STATES OF AMERICA, and I enclosed posters and newspaper clippings. Moreover, I had found excellent maps of Niagara Falls, and so I sent precise blueprints and all the engineering specifications for my "bridge." I said I was prepared to bring the entire apparatus with me by ship, but of course it would be much more convenient if the mayor knew local iron workers who might make stakes and clamps. Perhaps there was a source of seven-eighth-inch hemp ropes we could twist there into our wire? Did he know someone who would be willing to be my manager? I needed someone to make all these arrangements, who knew the local scene, who could handle publicity and announcements, an American manager and impresario. I would be most grateful were the mayor to suggest a man. Of course, I would expect to pay the usual 50 percent of net profits.

As soon as I sent the letter, I started putting together a kit. Some favorite poles, shoes, the heaviest rope stretcher, items perhaps not available in America that we could not do without. I went ahead and made steamer reservations for myself and my most able assistant.

I timed it accurately. The letter stating that the mayor himself was my man came three days before our ship was to sail. I cabled my delight, and set off for America the first week of March, 1901, the first year of the new century. For Niagara Falls!

Talk about fun! We set up a practice wire between smokestacks high above the deck. I walked to the measure of the pitching seas. In every weather I was on the wire. It was like beginning again! After I had mastered *that* stretch of wire, I felt that there was little more to learn. I was wrong, but anyway . . .

Let me make one thing clear. I never even had the opportunity to walk over Niagara Falls itself. My manager the mayor, when he absolutely could not avoid the question, would spout some nonsense about the technical difficulties of setting up exactly over the Falls. He was just lying. I would have had no trouble whatsoever stringing a wire over the Falls.

The fact is that officials of New York State and the United States would not let us do it. They said it would be a desecration of the natural beauty of Niagara Falls.

I still do not understand that. Mine is the most ephemeral of arts. We set up a wire, I walk, we take the wire down, and except for a few holes in the ground from stakes and a chipped rock here and there, no trace remains. The holes fill in, the rock weathers. *No trace remains.*

We set up down the gorge below the Falls. A group of nature preservationists tried to prevent us from doing even that.

Of course there were already bridges over the river, and mine was temporary, but they did not like the permanent bridges, either. They were opposed to all man-made structures near Niagara Falls.

They went out of their minds at the thought of what they called "stunts."

Niagara Falls was to be treated as an outdoor church! Take off your hat and bow your head. They do not understand! Niagara Falls is a *tourist attraction*. One of the greatest. A church, to be sure, but to understand churches they should visit Lourdes or Chartres or Rome. They ought to see how the *Church* uses churches to take in the tourists' francs and liras and marks and pounds and dollars.

Sacré Dieu! I have *never*, in any country in Europe, been forbidden to attach one end of my wire to a church steeple. Officials of the Church approach *me*, and now these Americans refuse to let me walk in their church.

"Would you forbid a world-renowned organist to play in your church?" I urged the mayor to ask. He did not see the parallel. Instead he tried to find out who had to be paid off— an eminently sensible approach, of course—but he said he never could find the right person. More likely, he found that it would cost more than he wanted to pay.

The best we could do was stretch the wire across the gorge at White's Pleasure Grounds. Later we took it farther down and stretched it over Whirlpool Rapids.

It was the last time I used rope. While waiting for my manager the mayor to make arrangements, I made a sport of walking up and down the guy wires of the railway suspension bridge. They were seven-eighths-inch steel cables. That is where I got the idea of changing to steel.

While I walked the cables I smoked good Virginia cigars.

Those cigars! They were by far the best thing I had found in America. The wine was terrible. I shall not even mention the food. I was afraid my palate and my stomach would be permanently ruined. But the cigars!

My bridge across Niagara Falls was the usual, a rope made of three one-inch ropes twisted together. It was nearly two inches thick and 1,300 feet long. A forest path. I wanted to avoid getting it wet. So we first took an inch rope across the gorge in a boat, and pulled it up to the level of the platform. We attached one end of the inch rope to a big drum and lashed the other end onto the big rope. Then four men started winding the drum to pull the big rope across in the air.

We stopped when the big rope was still 200 feet from reaching our side because the tension had become enormous. We were afraid that adding 200 feet more of the big rope fed out from the other side might be enough to break the small rope. Nobody seemed to know what to do, but to me it was obvious.

I climbed up on the drum and stepped out onto the inch rope. It was over the ground there, of course, but it would not have been fun if the addition of my weight had broken it. There was enough give. I came back, they tied the end of another inch rope around my waist, I took up my pole and walked out to the big rope. I kneeled down and tied on the end of the rope I had carried out. Then I turned around and walked back.

The newspapers called me a hero, but I did only what had to be done. I build bridges with very narrow, single-strand rights-of-way. They are meant for use, after all, for someone to walk on. If there are not many people who can, or will, walk on my bridges, this does not mean that they are not perfectly suitable as bridges for those of us who can and will.

There is at least one man—me—for whom walking out that small rope to rescue that big clumsy snake with its head poked out over the river—you see, I found it amusing!—for whom such a task is routine. It is not that there was nothing to it, that *anyone* could do it. No, I grant that it is difficult. I am, after all, highly skilled. Just knowing how to walk the wire is not even enough. I am also an engineer. I know about strengths and tensions.

There is another thing, I suppose, that I have not yet really talked about. The height. What is there to say? At Niagara Falls it was 180 feet on the Canadian side and 165 on the United States side. That does not matter. Once the height is, say, more than thirty feet above the ground, if you fall, you are dead or crippled anyway, so as I said, you do not fall and you do not even consider the possibility of falling. It just is *not* done. I never think about the height, except as an engineering problem, as a factor in determining the behavior of the wind and the wire. It is all very familiar to me.

Here is the point I am trying to make. If everyone walked the wire, then there would be no mystique about it. The limits would be well known, and the ordinary man would stay within them. No one would ever think much about falling or ever say anything about it except in bad taste.

And of course people would fall off all the time!

But, you see, no one would think that out of the ordinary, for it would be merely a part of walking the wire, and *everyone* would walk the wire.

Certainly people would think it tragic when young and promising walkers, their lives ahead of them, fell. On the other hand, it would be understandable when the weak and very sick let go. As for drunkards and daredevils, they should not have been on the wire in the first place. And when old men finally stumble and fall, is it not the way of the world?

It is just an accident that we do not all walk the wire. It could have been the normal way. Do we not have two feet to place on the line, two hands to hold the pole, and is it not even a matter of balance to stand up on the ground? Well then!

I never think about walking the wire. You laugh? On the wire, I never think about it. On the wire, I am, I do.

America made my name, but I was lucky to get back home—I mean, to Europe—with my shirt. I find it difficult to believe that my American manager, the mayor of Niagara Falls (who will continue to remain nameless in this account because I will not further contribute to his fame by linking his name with mine), this shyster, this mountebank, this clever crook, I do not really believe that he was responsible for the disaster that put me in his debt. I think he just took advantage of my stupidity.

I had planned my great walk—the first ever over Niagara Falls—to coincide with the Easter holidays. I admit that he did say to me that he was not sure that there would be very many people around on Easter. I replied that when they heard what I was going to do, they would change their plans and come to see me. He looked dubious, but said nothing more. Then was when I think he knew he had me!

Because, of course, as any American could have told me, Americans do not have Easter holidays the way we do when the streets of Paris are filled for a week with tourists from all over Europe. They do not write songs about April in Paris for nothing. It is beautiful.

Any American could have told me that it is *cold* at Niagara Falls in April. Fool that I am, I had looked at a map to find that Niagara Falls is at the same latitude as Marseilles. Well, then, it would be warm in April, I thought. I should have known that Lake Ontario is not the Mediterranean Sea, that the center of America has what is called a continental climate, which means that it is cold as Siberia for half the year. The half, alas, that includes Easter.

I noticed it was cold, although for a while it was unseasonably warm, something my manager kept congratulating me about as though I had been responsible for it.

So far as I could tell, he did not stint on publicity and announcements. Newspaper reporters were good to me, stories about me appeared in all the papers. My manager was worried, but I was not.

The day arrived and nobody came! Almost nobody, anyway. What to do? Well, it had been announced. It was cold but clear and there was no wind. I am a person who does what I say I will, and I knew I could do this. I conferred with my manager. He said to forget it, it would be a waste. We would do it later in the summer when we could get a crowd.

I looked at the newspaper reporters gathered around. If I did not do it, they would make sport of me. I picked up my pole and walked out onto the wire.

"Don't be a Goddamned fool!" my manager screamed at me. "You stupid idiot, get back here!" I froze. My mind was as clear as crystal. I did not even think about the insult. I thought about the fact that he was right. I walked backward to the platform again.

I turned to my manager and said, "Thank you for bringing me to my senses. I'll do it when there are more people."

He had not expected such cooperation. He took the reporters aside. The result was that most of them wrote that conditions had not been right. I would walk the wire later. My manager said it had cost him a pretty penny, and even then there was a note of sarcasm in some of the stories.

How was I to know that Easter is an at-home holiday in America, that people go to church on Easter Sunday and no-where else, that these *puritans* think it sinful to enjoy yourself on Sunday? If my manager did not tell me, which he finally did, after the fact. I found it difficult to believe even then with the truth before me.

"Why didn't you tell me?" I asked my manager.

"You seemed determined," he said.

It is true that I am a forceful man. At this juncture I was also mostly a bankrupt man. I was not sure that I had enough money even to pay passage back home, let alone to take along the 1,500 feet of new walking rope and 40,000 feet of one-inch guy rope, and all the other things it turned out that it was my side of the partnership to pay for. Of course, no one would buy them because no one else in America could use them.

I was getting chilled in my tights. Thin clouds crept over the sky and the air got colder. The few straggling spectators left. I looked at the wire again, and then went back to my hotel.

The next day we started taking down the wire. Before we finished it was snowing! I spent two days worrying about the weight of ice on the frozen wire. As soon as the weather cleared we pulled the big rope in.

Then followed a fabulously beautiful spring, with apple blossoms, balmy skies, as lovely as *la belle France!* It was still the low point of my career. I did not even have a woman!

My manager told me not to worry. There *was* a holiday when Americans did go out to celebrate. Niagara Falls would be one immense carnival on the Fourth of July. He got some engagements for me in Buffalo, New York City, Boston, Montreal, Toronto, and several other cities. My name was appearing in the papers, and in every story it was announced that I would walk over Niagara Falls on the Fourth of July.

As for that, I could not follow the negotiations. That is, I could never see what was really going on. The reporters were basically in favor of my actually walking over the Falls, and they related my remarks about the history and dignity of wire walking with great sympathy.

On the other hand, the columns of letters to the editor were filled with opposition. "Why don't you publish letters in favor of me?" I asked. They laughed and said there were none except from my manager. The next day they did publish a letter from him that everyone could see was self-serving.

Then there was an editorial suggesting that I make my walk over Whirlpool Rapids, which would be just as death-defying as over the Falls, and would not detract from the natural beauty of the Falls for those who wished to contemplate its pristine form. What they made of the observation towers on either side, the *Maid of the Mist* which steamed right up to its base, and the pleasure parks strung along the banks of the Niagara Gorge, I do not know. All I know is that they would not let me build a bridge over Niagara Falls itself.

Did it really matter where I put the wire? Not a tittle in Europe, I well knew. Wherever I put it, the European newspapers would report that I had done the impossible by being the first man to walk the wire over Niagara Falls. That would be quite enough.

Yes, I was looking ahead, counting my chickens before they hatched. I was desperately in need of funds. To get them, I had to make sure that the first crossing was followed with something even more spectacular, so I had a wheelbarrow made and my manager promised to let me push him across the wire in it. We could do that the next day, and then we would surely secure a crowd for a series of walks through the rest of the summer.

My manager had always stayed well back before, and I rather looked forward to taking him out on the wire.

I had even better than that in store.

Stilts! I had done some wire walking on stilts in Europe, but it was not my favorite thing. My trademark was running leaps on the wire, forward and backward. I had perfected back-jumps of fifteen feet in length. Quite amazing! To see me flying backward through the air over the wire.

On stilts I just walk. It is not very hard, but it looks totally impossible. So I set up a short wire and practiced walking on stilts. They were only three feet in length, but quite enough to give the impression of height. I am already a tall man, and on stilts look ten feet tall!

Then it was the Fourth of July. My walk was a bowl of cherries. I was magnificent! The toast of two countries. The Fourth of July *was* a celebration, like Bastille Day. At night there were fireworks over the Falls (I refrain from comment), and later I did a night walk with sparklers attached to the ends of my pole and a pack of Roman candles on my back that I set off at mid-wire. It was all very spectacular.

At last the Americans began to warm to my art. Did I say warm? It was 100 degrees Fahrenheit, which is 43 degrees Celsius, and that is *hot*. I was sweating like a pig, so much that my feet were slopping in my shoes.

My initial walk, the first across the Falls, was faultless. I was dressed in tights covered with spangles that caught the sun and made me appear to be clothed in light. I started out exactly at four o'clock, as advertised, and when I got to the center, where the wire was horizontal for 300 feet, I ran and leaped forward, and then leaped backward. I stood on my head, and then sat down in the very center of the wire. The *Maid of the Mist* steamed to a position directly below me, and

I let down a cord I had carried wrapped around my waist. They caught the cord and tied on a bucket containing a bottle of champagne. I pulled it up and drank it all, for I was dying of thirst. I tossed the bottle away, and lowered the bucket back to the deck of the *Maid of the Mist*. Standing up again, I ran along the wire until it started sloping up, then walked up the incline to the other side.

Both banks were black with people. Bands were playing, people yelling, and the crowd pushed up so close that I feared for my life as I approached the platform. As soon as I arrived, the fools grabbed me, set me on their shoulders, and paraded me through the crowd. Everyone wanted to touch me. The cheers were deafening.

It was rough, but yes, I enjoyed it. I deserved whatever they thought was the best way to exhibit their esteem. The passed hats were filled with money. My fame was assured.

As soon as I could get free, I returned to the wire and ran back to the other side in just under six minutes. Again I was carried on men's shoulders, but fortunately suffered no serious harm.

The newspaper reporters treated me magnificently. It *was* a historic event, and they recognized it. The only sour note was an editorial raising the ghost of Sam Patch, who years before had leaped from beside the Falls into the basin below. He had survived his first leap, but died on his second. They said that Sam had deserved to be dashed to atoms for his repetitive foolhardiness, and recommended that I take heed and not try my stunt again.

Stunt! I despaired of these Americans ever understanding.

Then after several weeks papers started arriving from Europe and I felt vindicated. My accomplishment was front-page news in France! It had good coverage everywhere. As I had anticipated, all the European papers reported that I was the first man to walk over *Niagara Falls.*

My visit to America put my name on the map. If I only earned enough to escape back to civilization from this barbaric land! But profitable as the Fourth of July holiday was, I still had not earned enough money to pay for the rope.

The next day my manager refused, after all, to ride in the wheelbarrow. Instead, I walked on stilts, which was very well received.

He promised to ride the wheelbarrow the next day, but again backed out. I was not concerned because I had thought of another scheme—the Grand Canyon. My manager discouraged me severely. Did I not know that it was a mile across? Of course, but I also knew that there was a place where I could walk a thousand feet from one side out to a pillar of rock. They would say, the European papers would report in headlines, that I had crossed the Grand Canyon!

It *was* a good idea, but my manager's contacts were all in the East, and I had to stay at the Falls because he controlled my purse strings. He said he definitely would ride in the wheelbarrow that coming Saturday.

Now Taylor enters my story and my life. Anna Edson (or Edison, she did not care how the newspapers spelled it as long as they printed it) Taylor. *Mrs.* Taylor, although in the American way I always called her Taylor. She called me Gravelet.

She was a widow, a schoolteacher from the West, and she had two grown children whose pictures she showed me. A boy and a girl, they had gone to California.

She was a pleasant, matronly woman. Not my type. It was not her age! I was nearing thirty at the time, but I knew forty-five-year-old women who were choice. No, it was her big round face, her ample cheeks, her size all around, for she was a big tall woman, and she weighed 180 pounds. Her upper arms were fat like a peasant woman's, and her thighs . . .

Taylor was the woman the spunky country maids I hired at my villa in Cannes later turned into. They would grin at me in the market, come up slyly and turn a hip into my groin while they talked. And roll their behinds as they walked away. Oh, I got along with them famously, but they were no longer my maids.

The day came for the wheelbarrow ride. I could tell the signs. My manager had no intention of joining me on the wire. I had no idea what he thought we were going to do, for it had been advertised far and wide, and there were large crowds on both banks. The time approached and he disappeared, as I had predicted. Then he reappeared with Taylor.

She was grotesque!

You remember those pretty little girls in petticoats, walking the slack wire? You remember Coquette, so petite and pert in her tights. Taylor was the antithesis of these.

It was not entirely apparent at first, because she was clutching a full-length cloak around her neck.

I saw at once what my manager had arranged. He need not have been so devious. I did not need to be tricked. I would have wheeled a cow across the gorge if she could be depended on to relax and sit still.

Now, apparently, I should have my chance! For my manager led Taylor up onto the platform, took hold of her cloak at the shoulders, and whipped it off, revealing . . .

I hesitate to say. I liked Taylor. I would protect her dignity, but memory can be cruel, and as the years have gone by I remember more and more the painful things. The puzzles in

my life are particularly painful, the more so as I realize that
they are never going to be solved, or at least not by me.

Taylor was a decent woman. Perhaps you have been to the
beach in recent years and have seen the results of the 1920s
"liberation" of women. Some of them might as well be nude in
those tight suits. Not that I object, far from it! But that is on
the beach.

You may forget or not know that thirty years ago, at the
turn of the century, a swimming dress was thought by many to
be as scandalous as nudity itself because it resembled nothing
more than a lady's underclothes, a kind of coverall with ruffles
at strategic locations. On the beach there was acceptance of
this umbrella wear even for wives and mothers, but on the
stage, in a pleasure park, right out in front of this crowd at
Niagara Falls, such dress suggested a less than respectable way
of life.

Taylor cringed visibly as the crowd responded, then she
seemed to forget them, smiled at me, and said, "Should I get
into the wheelbarrow now?"

It was obvious to her and to anyone near her that she was
not a woman of easy virtue from the music halls. My manager
had convinced her that this was what female performers on
the wire must wear.

I positioned the wheelbarrow on the wire over the platform,
stepped up and adjusted myself to the balance. A wheelbarrow is not like a pole, but if you concentrate always on keeping
the wheel on a knife edge, equal weights resting on either side
of the wire, you are as solid as stone. The faster you go the
easier it is to adjust for balance.

I nodded to Taylor to step up onto a stool and get in. I
refused to let anyone steady the wheelbarrow. I wanted to
wrestle it myself. Under my instructions she put a foot care-

fully in the middle, like entering a canoe, reached across with one hand to the other side, shifted her weight and sat down with her knees up, facing me, a serious look on her face but yet a smile in my wheelbarrow.

That she could follow instructions so well despite surely being under great stress encouraged me. So far, so good.

I tipped the wheelbarrow to the left and right and she instinctively moved to the right and left to keep her balance. She did not lunge. She did not seem overly worried. So far, very good.

"If the lady will relax, all will go well," I said

What would you have said in reply? Your first time on the wire, nearly 200 feet above Whirlpool Rapids, to ride in a wheelbarrow 1,300 feet across the Niagara River Gorge? Over the Falls?

Do not tell me. I already know. Your face would have turned white, your throat would have been too dry for speech, you would have nodded, and far from relaxing as instructed, you would have been as tense as the wire itself on which our wheelbarrow sat. I would have had to fight your stiff weight all the way across.

Not Taylor!

"Why, I feel just fine, Mr. Gravelet," she said, her smile broadening. She *was* relaxed. This large woman in white linen covered with red and blue ruffles and bows.

"I feel just fine," she said, *and she talked to me all the way across!*

I want you to understand that in this trade, in the world of circus performers, on the pole, the trapeze, the wire, there are some truly fearless people. They are literally without fear. Often they are very good, but because they have no fear they do not always respect the limits of what they can do. So they die.

I am wonderful, but I am not fearless. That is why I am alive today, sixty years old and still the best of them all, walking the wire now for forty-five years.

I tell you that by the time I reached the other side with Taylor I was sweating from more than the heat. I could not tell her to shut up! *Taisez vous, s'il vous plaît!* No, I did not know what she would say to that. I was scared to death. I was afraid that my manager had given me a crazy to take across in my wheelbarrow.

Thank God, Taylor was not, after all, a crazy. Thank God, because I knew—as surely as old Konrad had known when he turned that time to see Coquette already on the wire—I knew that as long as I stayed at Niagara Falls, Taylor was going to be part of my act. I did not want it. God knows how I did not want it! But it was and had to be.

You say I protest too much? I exhibit a typical Gallic predisposition for hyperbole? I could just have told her to go away?

Yes, objectively I could have. We French, however, besides being criticized for emotive excess, are esteemed for cold logic. All things considered, I needed Taylor, an American, and a woman, in the act. That was obvious from the cheers of the crowd when we started back, which after an hour we did, by popular demand!

I think right then it would not have been possible for me to refuse, even if I had thought she was a crazy. She drank lemonade, was good with the reporters—told them about her children as she had been telling me—and performed like a real trouper.

"No, no, never in my life before," she answered, laughing gaily. "Of course, if Gravelet," she had already become familiar and had dropped the *Mr.*, "would be willing to take me, I'd go right back across. It's a nice view and a pleasant ride."

I took her back across. This time she asked me questions and I grunted answers. I usually think about only one thing when I am on the wire, about what I am doing. That is, on the wire, my thinking and my doing are the same. I do not remember what I said to her.

"Mrs. Taylor!" my manager greeted her. "Magnificent!" He helped her down, fastened on her cape, and winked broadly and disgustingly to me behind her back.

Taylor turned and smiled and waved as *our* manager led her away. I raised a hand slowly in reply.

The one thing she had not told me was what in God's name she was doing in a wheelbarrow out on that wire.

"She came to me," our manager said. "She's tired of teaching school and she wants to make a name for herself. She wants to go on the lecture circuit!" he laughed.

"She talks enough for it," I said dryly, examining my cigar.

"Yes, she came to me and asked if she could take my place in the wheelbarrow. She had seen the advertisements, and she thought the crowds would like it better if it were a woman. Well, what could I do?" he said spreading his arms and grinning. "She was right. I'm not half so pretty!" He slapped his knee and guffawed just as we are taught in France that cracker-barrel bumpkins in America are supposed to do. One of my keenest disappointments in visiting America was in discovering how true the stereotypes were. Awful food, dreadful wine, overweening boorish, familiar, and disgustingly *friendly* strangers. Yes, and clever Yankees right out of Mark Twain's Court of King Arthur, capable of stroking you so skillfully that you purr as you are being skinned.

I was not amused, but I understand show business, and my sympathies were with Taylor. If it was logic and not fate that decided me, there is still no harm in dressing the mundane in

ruffles and bows. Otherwise, who would notice that the normal is the strangest of all?

Taylor, plain as mud, was an original. In no way that I could
tell different from any decent middle-aged woman of the
lower middle class. She was eminently sure of herself, she
knew what she wanted to do with no doubts whatsoever, and
she was not surprised in the least when she succeeded. If she
had shown no taste for derring-do for forty-five years (and I
do not *know* that she had not—there was a report in the newspapers that she had crossed the American continent from
ocean to ocean eight times, but she just laughed and winked at
me when I asked her about it), she did not think it unusual to
have chosen a dangerous profession now.

If she *did* think it dangerous. But of course she did. She was
perhaps foolish, but she was no fool. She had been a teacher
and had raised children of her own.

"But what do your children think?"

"They don't know," she laughed. "I haven't told them yet!"

Taylor.

She rented a small house in the town of Niagara Falls. I
lived—as always—in the best hotel. I say it was the best, but
considering the others, it was really the only hotel in town and
was far from what I was accustomed to.

I did not see her again until the next weekend. She arrived
this time on our manager's arm in the same outfit.

"How have you been?" she said as she got into the wheelbarrow.

I do not often come close to panic, but I could not again
bear her chatter while I was working. "Dear lady," I said,

creasing my brow, "I've had a headache but it appears to be gone now. I would so much appreciate it if you did not talk on the way across."

She looked crestfallen but nodded that she would be quiet. When we reached the other side she was her old effusive self. It was remarkable how she responded to the reporters and the crowds. As though she had been a personality all her life. Nothing nonplussed her. Rude and risqué remarks she simply ignored, or she reduced the speaker to shamed silence by staring at him. She was every bit the lady, wearing those absurd ballooning linen "tights" as though they were the latest in high fashion, that is, by appearing to be completely oblivious to what she had on.

Perhaps it was the school teaching. She was especially good with children, and was infallible in detecting little girls who wanted her autograph but were too shy to ask. Then "Gravelet! Gravelet!" she would shout, "this little man wants to grow up to be just like you, isn't that wonderful! Come now, and shake his hand," and I would bend down and do it.

In Europe I always remained aloof. The crowds there respected my privacy. I was set apart, and not just anyone could approach me. The American way is different. I had not been a success at it until Taylor took me under her wing. She treated *me* as though I were a shy little boy who had to be coaxed to bring his light out from under his bushel. I bridled, but I knew she was right.

After an hour again, we went back. Taylor started to say something, but I put on my deepest frown and she was silent. She was more than quiet, she seemed crushed. It was too much for me. Remember, I am a man who likes women. I liked Taylor. Just before we reached the other side I said, "Taylor, tonight you will go to dinner with me." I had meant to ask a question, but it came out as a statement.

Her homely face came alive with pleasure. "Yes," she nodded vigorously. Then we had arrived and were meeting the crowds.

"Here," Taylor said as she pulled me over to introduce an old man and woman, and she pressed a coin into my palm. I had time only to see that it was a twenty-dollar gold piece.

"What?" I asked, but she was already talking.

"Mr. and Mrs. Brown here are from *Nebraska,*" she said, "all the way from Nebraska, my home state! For their second honeymoon at Niagara Falls. Isn't that wonderful?" she said, nudging me.

"Why yes, that's splendid," I said, shaking Mr. Brown's hand. Then I remembered just in time not to take Mrs. Brown's hand, too. They giggle, these American women, if you kiss them on the hand, and they are—can you imagine!—shocked if you kiss them on the cheek. I soon stopped any of that kissing. Some of them make less fuss about going to bed with you than they would if you kissed them politely in public. Never mind. I was learning American ways.

I took Taylor to the hotel dining room. It was respectable enough, but I apologized as I led her in. "The food is not good."

"I'm sure it will be fine," she said, looking around with sparkling eyes. "Oh, Gravelet," she said in spontaneous delight, "this is all so new and wonderful to me."

Can you doubt that my heart went out to her, and why? I am what Europeans call a *gallant.* I rose to the occasion. Never mind that she was not an elegant woman. She was large and lumpy. Her hat was not askew but it *looked* askew. Her brown outer dress was cut the wrong way so that it emphasized her width.

No Frenchwoman would ever be seen in those sensible bootlike shoes!

This was Taylor, and she was, so far as I could tell—except for that tiny peek into her soul when she winced that first time she appeared *en costume*—never aware of how she appeared.

She was ugly, but so what? And after all . . . I am a Frenchman. Of course I like to dandle the pretty little girls, but I have a European appreciation of beauty. Some of the greatest courtesans were physically ugly women, but they had wit and sense and verve and intelligence and they knew how to please. I will not say that Taylor could have measured up to Madame de Staël, but if she had been able to procure an audience, she *might* have fascinated a king.

Actually, that is absurd. She was an original, of course; she had to be extraordinary to take so readily to my wheelbarrow. Otherwise, there was nothing unusual about her. She was a large woman of a certain age who had raised two children on her own by teaching school, and now through her own devices she was seated in the dining room of the best hotel in Niagara Falls with an extremely handsome Frenchman fifteen years her junior, a man exquisitely dressed, with impeccable manners, urging on her another glass of (bad) wine, and inciting her again and again to let go with the most deliciously deep belly laughs it had ever been his pleasure to hear.

I had *never* before heard a woman laugh like that. My god, it was a joy!

She got me to talk about my childhood from *before* I ran away. She reached out and held my hand when I remembered that I *had* missed my Mama terribly. I had never before confessed to anyone that after a few weeks I had tried to run away from the circus and that they had found me easily. I did not know where to go. They told me we were by then hundreds of miles from my old home, and I would never be able to find it.

A tear slid down her cheek, and she corrected my English.

The tears were soon from laughter. I saw to that. Once without thinking I patted her on the knee, and although she moved her leg aside she did not stop laughing.

I took out the twenty-dollar gold piece she had given me. She rolled her eyes up coyly when I asked about it.

"Oh," she said, "someone gave it to me." Then she laughed and leaned over with her hand on *my* knee to speak conspiratorially, tête-à-tête.

"Do you ever get gold pieces?" she asked. "I mean, from the crowd."

"In the buckets?" I replied. "Very seldom." The boys probably take them if there are any."

"Or our *manager*," she said significantly. "I was testing to see. Last week I was given three, and I gave them to *him*, and he never said a word about it to you, did he?"

I shook my head slowly. The manager and I, we kept close watch on the buckets. We divided it up together. Very seldom was there a gold piece.

"He took them," I said, shrugging my shoulders. "What did you expect?"

She laughed. "I knew by the way you looked when I gave it to you. Well, I can tell you, *he* collects a few. I saw him. Today, I did too." She looked around, took out a small embroidered purse, and opened it for me to see. There were eight ten-dollar gold pieces in it.

"Here," she said, taking out three and handing them to me.

I reared back and put my hands behind my back. "But they're yours," I said.

"They're *ours*," she said calmly. "Who did the people come to see? Come on, it was a hundred dollars today. That's fifty each. I've already given you twenty, now take your other thirty."

What could I do? That is, I am a *gallant,* but I am no fool. I took the coins, tossed them in my hand, and put them in my pocket. I leaned back and looked with renewed interest at my shrewd dinner mate.

"That Nebraska couple, they gave me the twenty-dollar piece," she volunteered.

"But how . . . ?" I asked.

"I watched our manager. You pick your people. You go up to them, speak of the danger, the expenses, of how glad you are that you can provide such a show for good people like them, and . . ."

"And," I held out my hand, "you hold out your hand in a certain way."

"You *knew* that," she laughed.

Of course I knew it. But I had not *done* it for years. I was above that sort of thing. I had not needed to.

"So why don't you do it?"

"How did you learn so quickly?" I asked, brushing aside her question.

"Oh, I catch on," she said with such gaiety and smugness and infectious glee that I laughed and laughed, really, for the first time in America.

There was a breeze off the lake and the night was not so oppressively hot. I hired a carriage to take us to her little house. Though she had talked a streak on the wire, now she asked and listened. She could not hear enough about my life in Europe.

Dimly in the back of my mind the caustic thought arose. "Why, the old thing wants to go back with me!" I did not let the absurdity and impossibility of her ambitions spoil the pleasure for either of us.

"The food really was very bad," I apologized, while acknowledging at her door that it had otherwise indeed been a wonderful evening.

"Well, you know, you're right," she said in one of those abrupt shifts from gay babbling to flat Western matter-of-factness. "It wasn't home cooking, that's for sure." She looked at me archly, I mean she cocked her head and raised one eyebrow and said, "You come here tomorrow night at six and I'll show you how good *real* home-cooked American food is."

She held out her cheek to be kissed!

I was so bemused that I was speechless. I kissed her cheek. She stood in the door and waved. I went back to the carriage thinking that I had something else planned for tomorrow night. Then I laughed outright. I would just have to put off my other lady friend's visit until another time. And, you know?, I did not mind. I positively looked forward to having dinner again with Taylor. Maybe the food would even be halfway edible, although I had my doubts.

Taylor. She was not a remarkable woman. Not really. Yet, who have I ever known who was her like?

Six o'clock! Is that what she had said? Of course, by then I knew it was so. Some Americans ate dinner at five-thirty, even at five o'clock! They ate quickly, everything on the plate at once, without talk and without wine. There were no wild Indians, no, but the land was full of barbarians none-the-less. Was there any hope of their ever becoming civilized? I doubted it. I still do.

Six o'clock. I did not know how long dinner would take, but I told the driver to come back in two hours. Eight o'clock. When the evening had just begun. It occurred to me that I could return to the hotel in plenty of time for my other rendezvous, but I was not so young that I piled women on top of one another any more, and so I dismissed the thought. To do a thing well you must give it your full attention, and my life was a sequence of performances done well. It had become a habit. The evening belonged to Taylor.

She met me at the door in a paisley print dress that was almost becoming. Her shoes were as near being slippers as any in America were permitted to be. She was flushed and smiling, always smiling, as she ushered me into the tiny parlor. Hardly had we sat down, though, when she bounced up and said, "You'll want to see my little house."

Sacré Dieu! This thing had happened before. Americans are an incredible race. I stood up and submitted to a tour of the even smaller dining room, the bedroom, then the kitchen full of American food smells (no herbs, no spices), and an enclosed lean-to attached to the kitchen for washtubs and a stack of wood to feed the kitchen range and the Franklin stove in the parlor. She indicated, I am not exactly sure how but I understood, that the privy was out back should I need it. The tour of this very small four-square house finished, we returned to the parlor. There were some small cakes and a slab of hard cheese on a tray. I tried to avoid looking at this poisonous display, but it was between me and Taylor, who sat in a rocker. Taylor herself was apparently uneasy about her attempt to provide *hors d'oeuvres,* and she leapt up again and said, "But it's after six! You'll want to eat." She ushered me into the dining room.

The evening before we had sat at table at seven. I held off the waiter and delayed half an hour with wine and talk. Our main course even then was served at seven-thirty, although I should have preferred eight. I had noticed that Taylor ate ravenously. She must have been famished by then.

In her own dining room I held her chair, but she laughed and said, "No, no. Sit down. I'll go to the kitchen and get the food."

She quickly brought in several uncovered dishes. The usual. Mashed Irish potatoes and the flour-and-grease sauce Americans call gravy. Green beans cooked to a mush (oh, for a taste of crisp green beans!) and fresh bread that did smell delicious. Pots of butter and apple jam were already on the table. She brought out steaming creamed corn, buttered turnips, and jellied beets.

Now, I thought, comes chicken in grease-soaked dough, fried so hard that you could never believe that this substance had once been meat, without taste except for an excess of salt. And you must eat it with your fingers.

Not at all. Taylor came out beaming with a large iron platter that she put down on a cutting board I had noticed sitting incongruously on the table. It was the most enormous *Chateaubriand* I had ever seen. It was sizzling.

"I'm from out West," she said, cutting the steak in two and urging me to hold up my plate. She took the other half herself and sat down, proud as Punch.

It was overcooked, but one cannot have everything. It smelled heavenly despite having no seasoning other than pepper and salt. She had cut a big bite, but paused. Taking her cue, I picked up my knife and fork, shifted them to the proper hands, and began to eat.

Taylor laughed and said, "I'll try, too! That's certainly a quicker way to get food into your mouth."

My face turned as red as the beets. I had never thought of it that way, but it is true that if you eat with your fork in your left hand and your knife in your right, you do not have to pause as Americans do to put down your knife after cutting meat to change the fork to your right hand. So while *I* had thought Americans ridiculous to go through this rigmarole, *they* had thought me greedy.

"No, no," I said calmly, shifting my fork to my right hand. "It's time I learned the proper American way."

"Oh, all right," she said, "but you'll have to stick your napkin into the neck of your shirt if you want to be American."

She said it so offhandedly that I did not know whether she was serious. Anyway, from then on, in company at least, I handled the cutlery as Americans do, but I did not stuff the napkin into my shirt.

It was a lot of meat. I protested politely, but she was marching right through hers, not sparing even a morsel of fat, and I knew I was expected to do the same. Potatoes and gravy, and then preserved peaches (spiced!).

After the meal, we sat at the table, stunned. I was nearly comatose. The hot weather, the time of day, and so much food.

She got up and said, "Now, about dessert . . ."

"Dessert? But I thought the peaches . . ."

"It wouldn't keep, and it needs a man to make it, anyway," she said.

I followed her out into the backyard, where she handed me an axe and told me to smash up a block of ice in a burlap bag. She started back into the kitchen, stopped to look at me speculatively, then said, "Use the flat side."

I crushed the ice. She brought out a tall metal cylinder. We scooped the ice into a wooden bucket, settled the cylinder in it, poured rock salt over the ice, and put on the lid.

"The man turns the handle," she said.

"Take off your coat," she commanded. The day was very hot. I sweated in shirt sleeves and we made ice cream. Of course, I knew how ice cream was made. It is not an American invention, but American ice cream is creamier and richer than the European variety, which when one thinks of it, is amusing. For what would French cooking be without sugar, cream, and eggs?

Taylor pulled out the paddles and scraped them off, but then handed them to me to lick. It is one of those tastes you remember, incredibly evocative, the rich creamy ice cream sharpened by contrast to the biting saltiness of the ice melt that had splashed onto the paddles as she pulled them out. We made ice cream often that summer, and although I have not experienced that taste again, not for thirty years, the mere thought of it evokes such poignant . . . memories. Painful ones? No. Just sweet and salty, in nostalgic juxtaposition.

We ate the ice cream on apple pie.

"It'll melt!" Taylor said with great alarm. "Eat! Eat! We have to eat it up!"

Finally I said, "No," and packed the rest of it back in the remaining ice in the bucket in a dark corner of the lean-to.

Taylor laughed.

I loosened my belt in discreet misery. I was going to have to visit the privy.

"You go outside while I wash up," Taylor said.

I sat there with the buzzing flies, imbibing more of Taylor's smells, not unpleasant, and wondered what now. It was still light. I looked at my watch. Not yet eight. I took my time.

Taylor had washed everything and was hanging up her apron. I stooped to step into her house through the lean-to door.

We returned to the parlor. Taylor was untypically silent. I had my coat back on and patted my breast pocket as a question. Taylor nodded assent, so I took out one of those wonderful cigars. I had the full paraphernalia. Case, cutter, matchbox. Taylor quickly provided an ashtray. I clipped both ends of the cigar neatly. Some men clip only one, but I want an even ash. I stuck the cigar deeply into my mouth, thoroughly wetting one end and then the other, savoring the stimulating bite of the tobacco leaf on my tongue. Then I rolled it in my mouth as I lit it evenly all around with a fine long wooden match. Tobacco. Those cigars. No, the European discovery of the New World had not been a total loss.

Taylor sat contentedly, smoothing her dress on her thighs with her hands. Later she let me know that she enjoyed smoking a cigar herself! I believe she was chattering. I was so content I did not notice, and when I had enveloped myself in a haze of aromatic blue smoke I was in another world. To be sure I nodded and hummed and said, "Is that so?" but it was easy to switch my mind to a French mode, and to hear the English as an exotic but unmelodious cacophony of sound.

"What?" I asked, coming out of my daze.

"There's been a man in a carriage sitting out in front of the house for an hour, and I think he's coming to the door."

I carefully put out my cigar and stood, smoothing down my coat in preparation for taking my leave. Then I looked at Taylor and saw that she was full of sadness to see me go, and without a pause in my brushing or a change in my demeanor I said, "Wouldn't you like now to go for a little drive?"

Taylor clapped her hands in delight. "I'll get my shawl," she said. "You go on out."

Good for her. I was beginning to think her intestines were not like those of other human beings.

I stood at the feet of the carriage driver, listening to him tell about the problems of his horse, or was it his wife? After a discreet interval Taylor appeared. We mounted the carriage and went for a ride.

I really had not looked around Niagara Falls much, other than as a problem in bridge engineering. Taylor, however, knew places she wanted to go for the view.

"It's getting dark," I said, settling back, not wishing to object, but merely stating the obvious.

"There's a moon," she said.

Yes, there was. It was full and bright, and the Falls were splendid in its light.

We got out and strolled. Taylor was ecstatic. "It's so beautiful," she said. "I've always dreamed of doing things like this."

I looked around. There were other carriages. There were couples strolling as we were. It dawned upon me. Honeymooners!

I looked down at Taylor, tripping along happily by my side. What a dreamer. No, what a *doer*, this strangely competent and determined and ordinary woman. I took her hand and we strolled along like two little children on promenade. She held my hand in the most natural way in the world. We walked and talked.

It was midnight when I took her home. I held her hand in the carriage too, but as we approached her house she took it back.

I went around to help her down from the carriage. At her door she again held out her cheek. I took her face gently in my two hands and kissed her softly on the lips.

It was Taylor's turn to blush. She waited until I was through, told me again what a wonderful evening it had been —"Two nights in a row!"—and stood at the door to wave as I rode off.

I took out another cigar.

That was Sunday night. I did not see Taylor again until the Wednesday performance. There was no reason for us to meet.

She seemed subdued as she walked through the crowd, but was her bubbly self as she got into the wheelbarrow. I had adapted to her chatter.

On the way back I noticed some silences, but avoided any contact with her soulful eyes. It was all too ridiculous.

Someone had stolen the wheelbarrow! Or they had pitched it into the river. The awful thing was that we did not notice its absence until an hour before the performance was to begin on Saturday. The wheelbarrow itself was ordinary, of course, and could have been easily replaced, but the wheel had to be specially made with a concave rim that could be seated on the wire.

That day the crowds—one on either side of the gorge— were tremendous. They had come to see Taylor wheeled across the gorge. And we had no wheelbarrow!

I looked at her. *Mon Dieu!* she was huge, but there was nothing else to do.

"Taylor," I said, "do you think you can ride on my back?"

"Oh!" she said. "Yes, I think I can."

"I can't hold you, I need my hands and arms for the pole. You'll have to wrap your legs around my waist and hold onto my shoulders."

"I think I can do it," she replied.

I nodded and turned around, and she mounted me to give it a try. She wrapped her long legs tightly around my waist and her arms around my neck.

"Not around the neck!" I gagged, and she quickly removed her arms to rest her hands on my shoulders.

"You can't hold on with your legs alone. Lean over against my back with your arms over my shoulders across my chest. Put your head forward, next to mine."

Her bosom, one would call it ample, was in the way, but she smashed against me. It was clear that she was not going to fall off.

Umph! She *was* heavy. And big.

She dismounted and we waited until time to start. I had carried people on my back before, but it was easier if they stood on your shoulders. I did not look forward to this walk.

"*Allons,* let's go," I said.

I picked up the pole, Taylor climbed on, and I stepped out onto the wire. It took only a moment to adjust so the center of gravity of our combined weights did not pull us over backward. After that it was just hard work.

More than I had anticipated. I spoke to Taylor. "Don't worry," I said, "but I'm going to have to rest. When we get to the center, I'll stop, and you'll have to get down and stand on the wire for a moment. Keep both hands on my shoulders and relax and it'll be all right. Can you do that?"

Taylor had never stood on the wire before. For good reason. She *wanted* to learn and I was not about to teach her.

"I think I can, Gravie," she said. Yes, she had begun using the diminutive of my name. No one else had ever called me Gravie. Intimates called me François.

When we reached the center I stopped.

"Careful now," I said. "We're quite secure. Hang onto my shoulders and let your legs slide back."

She was already doing it her way. She kept her left leg hooked tightly over my hip and reached back and down with her right, placing her foot solidly on the wire. Then she unfolded her left leg, and stood there behind me, her hands placed solidly on my shoulders. We were in perfect balance, and what a relief it was to be free of her weight!

"Excellent!" I said. "Taylor, I'm quite pleased."

I glanced over my shoulder at her.

That beaming face!

I turned back and rested.

"Gravie . . ." she said.

I turned in alarm at the strange tone of her voice.

Her face was solemn. She looked into my eyes and said softly, "I love you, Gravie."

Mon Dieu! Women!

"Get on my back," I said, bracing myself. I did not bother telling her how. She was doing quite well by herself. She slid her arms over my shoulders and supported her weight on them while those long legs came up and clamped themselves around me.

As we approached the other side and the roar of the crowd, she said quietly in my ear, "Don't be angry, Gravie. It doesn't matter."

I saw to it that we were separated by the crowd, and I did not carry her back. This was one trick that was not going to become part of the show, even if our manager had planned that it would be.

I walked back alone, did several of my famous backward leaps, one of a full fifteen feet, and I am gratified to say that they were appreciated. The papers the next day were filled with Gravelet, with *me* for a change, *my* stupendous prowess in carrying Taylor, a woman weighing 150 pounds (she weighed considerably more than that and they forgot the pole). They even mentioned the leaps.

I was in control again and immediately went out to order a new wheelbarrow.

When I returned to the hotel, Taylor was there. She looked as though she were reporting to the schoolmaster.

"Will you come to dinner again?" she asked, looking at me without expression.

I examined my cigar. My shoulders said it, that instinctive Gallic shrug. *Pourquoi-pas?* Well, why not?

"Only if you serve exactly half as much food," I said severely.

She looked blank, then smiled. Our eyes met—oh, how hers danced!—and we both laughed loudly. In the hotel lobby!

"And not until tomorrow."

She nodded, stepped back.

I nodded, too, and turned away. I am afraid she thought me impolite, but it was only a Frenchman defending his privacy. I did see her turn and wave from the door. I bowed and lifted my hand with the cigar in it an inch or two.

You think me crass? To toy with the affections of that noble woman? I doubt it was like that. Taylor knew where she stood. Should I have said no? Why? What difference did it make? It was inevitable that I would go to bed with her, once she had been on the wire. What did it matter? I had slept with hundreds of mature women. Everything that had happened to Taylor since she crawled into my wheelbarrow was more, infinitely more, than any woman like her could have hoped for or expected to accomplish. She had stood on the wire in perfect ease! So had she not earned it? I would make love to her. She would thank me for it. I knocked the ash from my cigar.

Of course, in October I would go away. Passage to Europe was already booked. Taylor was not included, *nor* was our manager. What a relief it would be to escape his clutches. I did not discount Taylor's determination. She might have something planned, but I thought not. My respect for her self-evaluation grew. Like me, she worked on the edge. It may have looked as though she were a reckless fool who did not realize how narrow the margins are, but I believe that she knew her limitations perfectly well. She had no foreign languages, for one thing, and she had been impressed with how I really did accept her instruction and improve my English.

"I wish I knew French," she said.

"It is not a language easy to speak well," I replied, and changed the subject.

We made ice cream almost every day that August, and even into September. Autumn came, and she introduced me to pumpkin pie. Pumpkins, food for pigs and cows! A small piece, a few bites, that was enough for me. She would eat the rest herself.

It was strange. We were subdued that second time I came to dinner. We sat in the parlor after the meal. I had dismissed the carriage.

I smoked my cigar and Taylor talked. When I finished my cigar, Taylor said, "Would you like to go to bed, Gravie?"

I nodded, stood up, and took her hand. She turned and led me to her bed.

That first time—I felt like a bridegroom! Although I could tell that it was not all that solemn an occasion. Later, Taylor would shriek with laughter as she told me the story, as she loved to do, of our first time together in bed.

She reached up and took off my coat and hung it up. Then she turned and glanced back at me. I unhooked her dress and helped her take it off.

"What if underneath I'd had on my costume?" she asked later.

She had on white pantaloons with pink ruffles and bows, the usual, not red, white, and blue.

I unhooked my shirt, removed my trousers, and we crawled into bed.

"In your long underwear!" she shrieked in the later telling.

"I wore what a decent man wears," I replied.

"In the summer!"

I refused to be baited. Besides, they were cutoffs.

I taught her to prepare the *Chateaubriand* rare.

"But it isn't *cooked*, Gravie," she said.

It did not stop her from eating her share.

She had carried a kerosene lamp into the bedroom, and now she leaned over to the table and blew it out. We lay there in the darkness, under a sheet. I was somewhat uneasy.

Not really.

I mean, after all . . . Here was this large warm woman next to me in bed. I put my arm back and she leaned her head on my shoulder. She was breathing easily. It was all right. There was no hurry.

We went to sleep!

Did I mention that Taylor had red hair. And freckles! The red hair was fading, but not the freckles. They stood out like paint flecks on her white skin. Even on her breasts and bottom.

"Naughty girl," I said, "naked in the the Western sun."

She blushed. Only a few times, she said, with other girls, in the creek, when she was small. It does not take much sun to make a freckle, and they never go away.

I awoke in the night. Taylor had removed the sheet and her undergarments and lay beside me, an unknown continent of naked flesh. She was unbuttoning the front of my union suit and this had awakened me. I slid out of it and turned to lie facing her.

"Gravie," she said laughing softly, "oh how I've longed to lay my hands on you."

She did, and I excited my hands on that skin of hers, smooth as silk, so much body and so soft. Her smell was some of cloves, but mostly like fresh-baked bread. As I maneuvered her into position, she laughed again and said, "I don't know if I still know how to do this, Gravie, it's been so long."

I was too intent to reply. She was, however, more than ready for me to enter her. She wrapped her arms and legs around me, her enormous breasts like a mountain range, her wide hips like the great plains, her soft belly like billowing clouds, I sank into the depths of this woman and lost all sense of my own being as my strength was spent. In short, I came instantly.

"*Pardon,*" I said as soon as I regained my breath.

"There, there, never mind," Taylor said, not relinquishing her hold on me. I could feel her controlling her high excitement. Her body began to subside.

I reached down, "Let me . . ."

"No, no," she said. "There'll be another time, plenty of time. I just want to hold you, feel your weight on me, feel you in me . . . oops!" she had punctuated her last remark by squeezing too hard, "well, *on* me, anyway," and she laughed again.

"I'm truly sorry," I said, not certain how to interpret her amusement and her words.

She took my face in her hands, kissed me, and then pulled my head down on her shoulder. "Plenty of time," she said.

To be sure, I was not worried. Within the hour I had her quivering with delight.

"Oh, Gravie," she gasped, I think I'll let go now," and she began to vibrate like a wire in a high wind until I thought the coming explosion would surely break the bed down. But she merely exclaimed in her softest voice, "Oh!" as she came.

She opened her eyes and smiled at me. By now I had re-lighted the lamp. She was a big fat woman. She did not have a pretty face. It had not retained the smoothness, the plumpness of her body, but was lined, and the skin, like that of her hands, was coarse. Double chins, to be sure, but also jowls. The ugly face of used-up peasant women the world around. But Taylor was not used up, oh no!, far from that. Her common face was striking and took on a rare beauty, because it was the face of a happy woman.

"I am so happy!" she exclaimed. Everything about her—her radiant smile, the bounce of her walk, the boom of her laugh, and the generosity of her giving herself to the crowds—showed it.

Need I say that it was *very* good for business?

Taylor was insatiable. I do not mean that she was never satisfied, for she seemed capable of coming to climax almost at will. Nor was she one of those poor mentally sick women who need sex the way others must have opium. No, she simply took immense pleasure in the act. I needed but touch her anywhere and she was aroused. No matter how many hours we dallied, she never tired.

We went at it with hammer and tongs!

"Gravie," she said to me the second night, in that speculative voice that I listened to with caution, for I had learned that there was nothing this woman might not say. "Gravie," she said running her index finger back and forth on my chest, "do you always do it this way?"

I thought it best to remain silent.

"I mean, this is the way my husband did it. You know," she laughed, "up on top and wham, wham, and that was about it."

I kept quiet.

"Gravie . . . I thought . . . don't Frenchmen do . . . other things?"

Then it was my turn to laugh.

"Bad girl!" I said. "And a respectable widowed lady like you, too!"

Taylor blushed—through it all she blushed so easily—but she persisted.

"Yes, but Gravie, *don't* you do it other ways?"

I taught her all I knew, all I had learned in all the countries of Europe.

"No! Come on," she would say in a flat, sardonic voice. "Nobody does *that*. You're just making it up to try to shock me." Then came the laughter that started in her belly and ended with wild tickling and tears. "We don't *have* a trapeze," she bellowed. "What a pity!"

That immense woman! She had the agility and flexibility of a contortionist. If I had, however, the thought now and then that she *could* learn to walk the wire, I suppressed it.

As I look back on those two months, August and September in that first year of the twentieth century, 1901 (and I have looked back many times in these thirty years since), I do not recollect it as the happiest time of my life. It was far, far from that. I was worried about my future, I was trying to escape my American manager, and I fretted about the problems of shipping my gear and getting it set up again in Europe. And I was puzzled by Taylor.

I have no doubt but that it *was* the happiest time of Taylor's life. Moreover, I can say without equivocation that there has not been (and will not be in the future) any other time in my own life when I have had more fun. Just plain hilarious fun. More fun than a barrel of monkeys. With Taylor.

Taylor was never crude, but she was totally uninhibited. I did not really know how seriously to take some of the things she said. When I bragged to her once that I had done every act on the wire but that of sexual intercourse, she said, "Oh, Gravie! Let's do it!" I believe she was serious, and, you know, it so engrossed me as a problem that I nearly took her up on it. We could have gone out during the dark of the moon.

"It already was about as much as I could do to keep from coming when you carried me across on your back," she teased. She had never said another word—since that time she stood on the wire—of love.

She had not made love for eighteen years! Not since her husband had died.

"But," I said.

"Goats butt," she said, interrupting me.

"But surely there were men . . ." I persisted.

"There are always men," she said sharply. "But a widow schoolteacher in a small town? With two little children to raise? Ha! Of course there were willing men, but not to marry me, and that was the only way I could have gotten a man in my bed without getting a ride out of town on a rail." She did not sound bitter. Only firm when she went on to say, more, I think, to herself than to me, "Now I do what I want."

One day Taylor threw the fear of God into me. "How would you like to have a baby?" she asked.

"*Non!* Have you not been taking precautions?"

She looked at me coldly. "I thought you Frenchmen knew about such things," she said.

She was sitting cross-legged on the bed. An immense pear-shaped nude, like the prehistoric figurine of the Venus of Willendorf I had seen a picture of in the newspapers. They had dug it up in Moravia. Ancient man, they said, worshiped it as a goddess of fertility.

"With me you couldn't tell until it was too late, could you?" she laughed without humor and slapped a hand on her belly.

Splat! Splat! Splat!

She watched the workings of my horrified face. "Don't worry, Gravie," she said, in a tired relenting voice. "I'm not pregnant. God knows I wish I were. I haven't used a thing, but nothing happens." She looked at me slyly. "Maybe it's you."

Jesus Christ! She could turn a thing on a man. No woman ever learned to provoke me the way Taylor did. She did not have to learn, it was natural to her.

"But I would like to have your baby, Gravie," she said wistfully.

These women. They *all* want to have a baby. But what on earth for? It is the easiest thing in the world. They talk of how brave it is to have a baby, but it does not even require courage. Once the fertilized egg is caught in the current it is drawn inexorably down to the river's mouth where the baby *will* come forth, courage or not. Bravery is not the issue, there is very little a woman can do or has to do once she gets pregnant.

All that *merde* about men being envious of women because women can make babies. That the artistic efforts of men, that their paintings and concertos and poems and wars are only because they are deprived of the inner creative power to produce life.

What utter nonsense! It deceives only women, to their eternal subjugation. Thank God men cannot get pregnant and have babies! This makes clear to them something few women can ever comprehend—that creativity requires *work*. One must study and practice, learn skills, go through long apprenticeships . . . Work! Work! Work! And think and plan and structure. A man must be an engineer! He builds his bridges. They do not form naturally in his body like a turd!

You think of Raphael, of Racine, of Mozart. You just think of me! I am what I have made myself. I am what I *do*—a work of art.

Art follows nature some say. Bah! Art is *against* nature. Nature is to walk on the ground, to avoid work and grow fat. Art is to walk the wire. To take what you have and shape it, mold it to an ideal form. It is to hold yourself ever in suspense against the natural forces, to challenge the way stones fall, to take the chaotic sounds of life and force them into ordered beauty.

I do not say a sunset does not have its beauty. But it is not a work of art. Of course a rosy-cheeked child is a joy to behold. But any country wench can make a baby. All she has to do is spread her legs.

Taylor had always wanted to do something. Poor woman, as a girl she had wanted to be a cowboy. (So, at one time, had I.) But there was not much she could do against nature when all the world knew and expected her to be what she was. She completed school. She went away from home to a larger town to teach school. She was big enough to make the older boys mind.

She married a young lawyer who came to the town. She was stronger than he. Do you know, he died of tuberculosis, an aristocratic disease! When I remarked on this to Taylor she gave me a look of worldly fatigue and said, "There was a lot of blood."

She sat pensively, naked in her bed. "For eighteen years I tried not to think about sex." Then she whooped. "What if they could see me now!"

I shook my head.

"Taylor," I said, "no baby."

"I reckon not," she said carelessly. "Maybe I'm too old."

Taylor did not tell me how she had come to be in Niagara Falls. I asked her and she just laughed and said she came to see the sights and there I was in spangled tights.

Our manager told me. He was in partnership with a man who had ridden the lower rapids below the Falls in a barrel.

This man had also swum the rapids. It was not a stunt that made very much money because it was hard for spectators to watch, and it was too dangerous to repeat. They exhibited the barrel and the daredevil gave a talk. Very small-time stuff.

What my manager had in mind was for someone to go *over* Niagara Falls in a barrel! Sheer madness. Naturally, his man who had ridden the rapids and knew what it was like had no intention of doing such a suicidal stunt. So they had advertised in Western papers for a bronco rider who would be willing to ride the rapids. They said nothing about going over the Falls, they were going to spring that on him later.

Taylor answered the advertisement!

Before they could get on with that, however, my letter from France arrived. The mayor saw the potential in my proposal —thousands of people on either side of the gorge could watch a man walking the wire—so he forgot about the stunt with the barrel.

After I arrived, though, there was the wheelbarrow. Yes, yes, he said, he would do it if nobody else would. Nobody else would, not even the man who had ridden in the barrel. I flatly refused to take a volunteer from the crowd. You can get a real crazy if you take that kind of chance. Volunteers, I stressed, have to be planted.

He then remembered the letter from Taylor and wired her to come, but he did not send her any money for train fare.

"Why didn't you ask for money in advance?" I reproached her when all this came out.

"I didn't think about it," she said.

"Why did you sell your house?"

She laughed. "I needed money if I was going to go to Niagara Falls, didn't I?"

I refused to get caught in her circles. Her idea of a joke

always seemed to me to be too much at the expense of good sense.

"I thought about my life, Gravie," she went on softly, "and I thought to myself that I could teach school in Niagara Falls, or somewhere else in the East, just as easily as I could in the West. I'd been in the West all my life. Why stay? Matthew was gone. The children were gone. I'd had enough of the West. I decided this was as good a time for a change as any, and it wasn't as though that property was something to hang onto. The house wasn't as good as this one. It wasn't worth beans."

"You're renting this house?" I asked.

"I'm all right," she said firmly.

I knew that our manager had caught on to her collecting from the crowds, because he lectured me about it. I told him haughtily that I did not do that. Then I did do it whenever I thought of it. Taylor continued, but had to give most of the coins to our manager.

"I keep enough to live on," she said, which made me ask sharply what our manager was paying her. She would not say. Nor would she take money from me. I left coins in the pot where she hid them in the kitchen, and I bought groceries.

"Don't worry about me, Gravie," she said. "I'll be all right."

I am not a shit. When I started seeing Taylor every day, I did not continue seeing other women. That is, I stopped seeing the one I had an arrangement with. Yes, she had begun to worry about her husband finding out anyway (why do I report this so scrupulously?), and no, I was not ungracious to the one or two enterprising girls who schemed their way into my bed back at the hotel. But when I go with a woman, I go all the way.

I did not move in with Taylor, although I stayed with her all night on several occasions. She never came to my room in the hotel, but that was her choice, not mine. She said people would not put up with it, and I took her at her word, although the management never complained about my guests.

Taylor was my woman and I treated her as such. We were a couple. I did not sneak around or deny our relationship, I never did with a woman, which in fact is sometimes the best way to conceal. Even though I had nothing to hide. Nor am I protesting too much.

Taylor and I were together everywhere. We saw all the sights (this is a standard routine when one has a woman). We had a favorite carriage driver, a laconic old man who chewed tobacco. He and Taylor had me try it under their tutelage— Taylor as a Western woman having learned to chew in her youth. She laughed but the driver just spat when I found it was not for me.

We went out to dinner, of course. To concerts and lectures and stage shows, all the many diversions provided for tourists and honeymooners who found that leisure provided more time than they had things to do.

We went to Buffalo to the Pan-American Exposition, and there we shopped for clothes. Taylor was alert to every nuance of my reactions, so I sat in this shop and that while she looked and modeled, and without my ever having to be so gross as to point a finger, she outfitted herself in the best style Buffalo could offer. She herself saw the difference.

"I never knew what to buy, or cared really," she said, "until I met you."

We were an elegant couple. I looked particularly chic in my ruffled shirts and suit jacket cut short in the latest Parisian style. In any capital in Europe, people would have turned to look at us only in admiration and respect, for Taylor had adopted my style of carriage and demeanor, and we could have passed for the very rich if we had not been known for the performers that we were.

But in America the people are jackasses. They would turn and point and laugh. Not everyone, no, of course not, the majority were polite. Often curious, but not derisive. Never-the-less, there were more than enough who brayed, and when they did everyone else smiled.

No matter how well caparisoned, Taylor had a homely face and was fat. She looked more than her forty-five years. I looked twenty-five, so youthful that no one would have believed I was nearly thirty. We looked . . . mother and son. Yet obviously we were lovers. For I do not stint. I offered her every courtesy that was her due. A woman who gives herself to a man, who loves a man, who accepts a man as her lover and becomes his mistress, she has a right to be treated with respect and consideration by that man. Courtesy comes first, but more than that, a thousand little attentions, touches of the hand, a mounting of the guard on every walk and at the passage through every door. Fond looks, sweet words, kind and affectionate attentions all.

This mode was second nature to me. I have never failed to please a woman. Taylor knew that I was sincere, that she was being treated as a woman should, and no one who observed us could fail to see.

Did I love Taylor? In my fashion. Did I not just say so? I made love to Taylor. It was there for all to see.

Our manager hooted. He gave me broad winks, slapped his knee, and asked obscene questions. This did not touch me. His real sentiment was incredulity. He knew I had my choice. He took me aside. "How could you . . . with *her*?" he asked.

I did not kill him. The age of chivalry *is* past (it was never present in America), and my manager was a fool. I smiled and waved off his questions. The weeks passed and he grew suspicious. We were obviously up to something. I felt I had to give him an explanation he could understand.

"Don't you think it's good for business?" I asked one day.

He looked blank, but then put his hand to his chin. "Oh," he said.

Thereafter when he saw us together he would grin and try to catch my eye, moving his thumb and forefinger together as though counting money.

"What does *that* mean?" Taylor asked, catching sight of him once.

I told her.

"That's what I thought it meant," she replied, "but I thought maybe it meant something else I didn't know."

We walked along. "You're right," she said pensively. "I'm sure it *is* good for business."

She left her question unasked. I found occasion just then to take her intimately by the arm. As she stepped off the walk onto the street I looked down warmly into her eyes with a smile of contentment on my face. She had her answer.

Of course I loved Taylor. I am not a shit. I do not stint. When I go with a woman I go all the way.

Taylor did allow me to pay for some of her new clothes, I give her that. She was not so hidebound in that petty lower-class ethos of refusing any gift whatsoever because of being so close to the line of poverty that any generosity on the part of a friend looks dangerously close to charity. The first time we went into a shop together and she chose an outfit under the guidance of my approving eye, I rose from my chair, put my hand on my wallet inside my coat, and walked without haste over to the manager with such authority that all Taylor could do was let me pay. She was so observant, so attentive to me, so sensitive to my moods and attitudes, that I could not help but continually approve her behavior. It is not that her personality was absorbed in mine, for she would suddenly guffaw at a fitting, hoist a skirt, and announce in a loud Western drawl, "Gravie! What do you think of *this?*"—a petticoat of black silk with many red bows. She knew that that embarrassed me, and it sometimes scandalized an elderly fitter, but it was within the realm of acceptability in the milieu of man and mistress, something Taylor seemed instinctively to know. She played the role so well that for long periods of time I simply failed to notice that she was ugly, fat, and old.

Fifteen years my senior. She *was* old enough to have been my mother, but the reality of the underlying relationship was of schoolmarm to pupil. She started teaching school about the time I started school. I would have been—had I ever finished—one of the big fifteen-year-old boys she knew so well how to corral when she was thirty. This was more than just a background. Taylor never forgot anything I said, and later at appropriate times—or even in my lights highly inappropriate times of intimacy—she would remember and give me a lesson in proper American speech.

Taylor decided which clothes I should buy for her. Enough to make me understand her worth. Then she went back to buy more on her own. To hold them, she got a new wardrobe to sit in the corner of her tiny bedroom.

I showed my worry, but we French do not discuss our friends' finances, or certainly not with them. Still, I could not help but remark in dismay on a fur coat she purchased.

For a moment she looked frightened—I say there were very

few chinks in her armor—and then she said, "Oh, you know it is very cold here in winter, and the price is better now. I don't want to be cold."

I avoided her eyes. My departure was scheduled for October 10th. We had twenty more days together.

"I won't buy anything more, Gravie," she said. Then in that flat tone whose import I never fully comprehended because it concealed all emotion except stoic forebearance and yet was not always serious, she said, "There won't be any reason to. Anyway, I can't. I'm about broke."

I said nothing then, but a few days later I continued the conversation. "So what are you going to do?"

She picked it up at once. "I paid the rent on the house for a year when I moved in, so I'm all right there. I'm not really broke, I just mean that I've spent all the money I brought with me. I've squirreled away enough to last until next summer."

"And then?"

"Oh," she said offhandedly, "I'll still be performing."

I looked my question.

"Tomorrow," she said, "I'll show you."

The next day she took me to the cooper's. In the corner of his shop stood the barrel. It was nearly as tall as I, bulging in the middle and tapering to either end. Taylor pulled over a stepladder so I could get a good look inside.

"This is stronger than the one they used through the rapids," the cooper said, "and there is more padding."

The cooper tipped the barrel up to show the false bottom. "We'll put an anvil in here," he said, "to keep it upright in the water."

Taylor stood back looking at the barrel. She was chewing a straw she had picked up from the workshop floor.

"I've been in it a couple of times," she said. "Fitting."

She assumed that I knew what it was all about. Of course I did, but I had not known that our manager had gone ahead with his barrel scheme. I stared at the barrel, fresh new oak staves, shining iron hoops. It was unreal. This early fall September afternoon. Dust motes drifting in bright sunbeams filtered through a dirty window into the shop. The cooper. Taylor watching me, the straw sticking from her mouth, and there the barrel, ready for violent action, an alien entity in this calm and orderly place.

I felt a chill. It was quiet today, but had the wind been right we could have heard the muffled roar. The Falls were over there just to the east. I could hear in my mind the thunder, the rumble, and feel the shaking ground. The water as heavy as lead and the spray like buckshot, the mist rising up. The current running fast, the smoothness of the standing waves showing like an engineering diagram the immense power of millions of tons of water, flowing, then breaking in a rush, the noise and overcoming urgency, the power and speed, taking everything in its grip to draw all inexorably into the plunge, free, over the Falls, to drop more than 150 feet to the basin below to be whirled and churned and sent back under the falling water, buffeted and blasted and tossed until at last the flotsam escapes the whirlpool and drifts on down, either to the shore, or on for another wild ride in the rapids below the Falls.

Taylor. In the barrel.

The iron grip of irresistible frenetic action takes hold of anything that floats past a certain line in the river above the Falls. Boatmen flirted with that edge and sometimes were swept over. Several people had gone over the Falls, in boats, in the water. None had survived. None had gone on purpose.

I had witnessed one staged "shipwreck." A decrepit and

condemned Great Lakes steamboat had been procured by some promoters, who advertised that it would be sent over the Falls, a "Ship of Fools," its decks populated by such wild animals as panthers, wildcats, bears, and wolves. In fact, they managed to gather a crew of two bears, two raccoons, half a dozen mangy stray dogs, and a goose. Human passengers were taken on the boat and discharged well above the danger point. Then the vessel was set loose at the mercy of the raging waters.

The bears, I am happy to say, jumped into the water just as soon as they were uncaged, and swam to safety in the woods along the shore. The boat was soon swept over the Falls and the other animals perished.

At the time I was not so much struck with the barbarism of the enterprise. After all, I had known bearbaiting, bullbaiting, dogfighting, cockfighting, and eyeball-gouging wrestling matches all my life. I had seen bare-knuckle boxing in America. No, as those poor animals plunged to their doom, I was envious of the crowds. The newspapers estimated them at 30,000 people, and I am sure there were at least 15,000.

How many could be expected to watch Taylor go over Niagara Falls in her barrel? How did our manager expect to make it pay? What were the chances of Taylor's surviving alive?

I thought of that goose, its neck stretched and head down, feet braced on the deck. I turned a look of shock and horror onto Taylor.

She had been waiting. She chewed the straw, shifted it in her mouth. "Got to do something, Gravie," she said. "Anyway, that's what I came here for in the first place."

I nodded. How could I object or argue? Taylor had never said anything to me about my going or staying, that is, she remarked now and then that the time was approaching, but she never asked me to stay.

That she did not want me to go, that she would have happily ridden in my wheelbarrow across the gorge from now to kingdom come, I knew without having to be told. Our manager had made a proposal, and his offer was quite generous, if it could have been trusted. It could have been worked out. We would perform six months a year at Niagara Falls. From mid-October to mid-March we would travel to cities in the South and to California and Mexico. He had even looked into the matter of the Grand Canyon, and said something could be arranged there. I could build a reputation in America as great as I could in Europe.

Of course it could have been done, but I was not an American and had no intention of becoming one. My notoriety in America was and would be one of spectacle. They thought of me as a daredevil, a crazy man, not as the artist I was. In Europe, recognition would be commensurate with critical comprehension of my skill. I did not want to mingle with the mobs. In Europe we all know our place. In a special sense, to be sure, but significantly, what I found unacceptable in America was just that thing that drew so many immigrants to its shores. Freedom. There was *too much* freedom there. Freedom and equality. People thought so well of themselves that they believed themselves to be the equal of anyone. They impose on you. They exaggerate their own worth and discount yours. I am not an egalitarian.

One bumpkin even bragged that he could walk across the gorge, and grabbed up a pole and started out before I could stop him. He kept his balance but froze fifty feet out. I took pity and went out to guide him back. Then his friends counted him a hero! It got in the newspapers that he had walked all the way across!

I have known men who were shot from cannons, who dived from high platforms into shallow tanks of water, who went into the cages of lions, who leaped from great heights tied to the end of a rubber rope. In all these feats there is required a modicum of skill, but somewhere a line is crossed on the other side of which chance and luck are more important than anything you have learned to do. It was perfectly apparent to me that riding the rapids or going over the Falls in a barrel was well on that side where success and survival depend not on you and your skill, but on slim chance and the grace of God.

"Taylor," I said, after she had shown me the barrel, "you really do intend to do this thing?"

"Yes," she replied, staring straight ahead.

I returned to my room in the hotel and spent the evening designing barrels. The next morning I collected Taylor and we returned to the cooper's.

He was stubborn at first, but then either he saw that I knew what I was about or, more likely, he realized that it was worth his time to go along with me. One way or the other I tamed him and took charge. I was careful to praise his barrel for what it had been designed to do, which was float down the rapids. Now *we* had to design, I told him, a barrel that would withstand a vertical plunge of more than 150 feet over the Falls.

We took apart the barrel he had built. It was sturdy, but I worried about its collapsing, so recommended installing internal supports. They had to give as well as hold, for if the cask were too rigid it would break. The cooper's barrel had handles within for the rider to grip, but they protruded. Taylor could have cracked her skull. I substituted straps.

In the end we built an entirely new barrel, one that satisfied me. It was not so tall as the original, but still tapered at the ends. I used the cooper's idea of having an anvil in its base to keep it upright in the water.

Taylor, you can imagine, took a great deal of interest in this. I teased her for an old schoolmarm, but was delighted to find her to be a woman with a considerable degree of mathematical intelligence, and we were closer during those days than we had ever been before.

When the new barrel was finished the cooper wondered if we ought to test it by sending it over the Falls.

"With what in it?" I asked with some annoyance. "And why?"

In matters like this you do not do tests. Suppose I were going to do a difficult walk. Would I have a trial run first? What nonsense! I was an engineer and I knew the barrel was right. It might not survive the fall, it might hit a rock, but if anything man-made could survive that trip, this barrel would. There was no need to test it.

When you build equipment to withstand a certain stress, how foolish it would be to take the chance of sundering its integrity by subjecting it to an unnecessary trial. If your theory is correct, you do not need to experiment.

Our manager, however, was taken with the notion of a trial. Unknown to Taylor and me, he had the original barrel put back together. The next weekend, to some fanfare, he towed it out into the river and released it to go over the Falls.

He put a cat in it!

The barrel floated like a cork, rode high over the lip of the Falls for all to see—and so it was a good idea, because the newspapers reported on the fearsome sight—and bobbed up unharmed at the base of the Falls.

The cat, battered from one end of the barrel to the other, was dead. This was unfortunate for the cat and, as it turned out, for Taylor. Because the newspapers reported that it was her little pet cat that she herself had put in the barrel. Our manager denied spreading the story, but probably he had. Also, it was one thing, apparently, to send some stray dogs over the Falls in a derelict boat, but it was quite another to send one's pet cat to its death. Taylor did not even have a cat; she had an aversion to them, and said so. This was transformed into the story that she had disliked her cat and was glad it was dead. I have noticed this before: If you do undertake the truly death-defying stunts, people prefer you to be very tough, harder and coarser than the ordinary run.

"Why are you doing it *now?*" I asked Taylor. "The weather is getting cold. There won't be many tourists in October. Why not wait until next summer?"

"If I do it now," Taylor said, "I can go on a lecture tour this winter. Then next summer, when I go over again, there'll be a big crowd."

Again!

"Taylor," I said, "you cannot do this thing twice."

"Why not?" she replied.

I believe that, intelligent as she was, she really did not understand. You can walk the wire thousands of times in a lifetime, but you go over Niagara Falls in a barrel only once.

Our manager had in mind Taylor's going over the Falls every summer, on the Fourth of July. "With you running out on us, we have to do something," he said with an immense shrug, a parody of my own French mannerism that made me boil every time he aped it. I looked at him scornfully and refused to be engaged.

It was poignant. October is my favorite time of year. It comes, I suppose, from my childhood reading of the wonderful Edgar Allan Poe. "In sere October . . ."

The changing colors of the trees were spectacular that year. Taylor and I became very tender with one another. The cowboy wildness of our earlier sexual experimentation calmed to gentle care. We were soon to part in many ways.

On our last walk on the wire, Taylor did a trick I had taught her. In the middle of the wire I stopped and she stood on her head in the wheelbarrow. There were not many spectators and it was not even reported in the newspapers, but it pleased Taylor to have done it, and it absolved some of my guilt from not having taught her to walk. At least that once, she had been a real part of the show and had done something more than ride in the wheelbarrow like a sack of grain.

Then there was a week to wait, with nothing to do. Monday was dreadful. There was nothing to talk about. What was I doing with this madwoman? Early Tuesday morning, after a sleepless night at the hotel, I threw some clothes into a bag and rushed over to Taylor's house.

"Quick," I said, "pack for four days."

"But I . . ." Taylor said. "Four days?"

"We're going to New York City on the morning train. Hurry! We've got only four days. We'll have to be back Saturday."

We were soon in the carriage on the way to the depot, and just caught the train to New York City.

I had not spent much time there myself—and it was Taylor's first time—but I knew what to do in a big city. Taylor's old gaiety returned. We saw the sights, I spent too much money on the latest fashions for Taylor—but of course it was a gesture of defiance, an announcement to the gods that this woman intended to survive, and wear these clothes, after the fall . . .

"I'll be too fat to get in the barrel!" Taylor laughed as we ate from every street stall during the day and then dined sumptuously at night.

Yes, I remember in great detail what we did and said. So what? It was an interval. *Pastorale*. It is not really a part of this story, is it? It was just a way of getting from Monday to Saturday. Because those days really had no reason to be, and we had no role to play. Had we been marionettes, we could have been hung up on our strings, the curtain pulled to darken the stage, and then on Saturday, our strings pulled, we could have been jerked into life and our bodies dumped grandly on the brightly illuminated stage.

Our manager was frantically waiting for us when we arrived at two o'clock Saturday afternoon. Taylor was scheduled to go over the Falls at four o'clock. He rushed us to his carriage and we set out for the Canadian shore. We had seen him in this state before, and I was pleased that Taylor's response to such intemperate lack of self-control was like my own. As people about us permitted themselves to become hysterical, Taylor and I grew more calm. I do not know how Taylor learned it—from schoolteaching most likely. I was that way because I could not indulge the luxury of uncontrolled behavior if I wanted to live. It was my observation that the further away a person was from direct participation in a difficult or danger-ous action, the more frantic he was capable of being. Certainly our manager was out of all danger, and as we rushed along— Taylor now in his grasp—he too calmed down. We had re-turned and there was no sign that Taylor had any intention but to go through with it.

He did have a job to do, after all, and he was a professional somewhat like us. When we reached the dock he quickly ush-ered Taylor into a room to change into her outfit. Then she was exhibited to the crowd. We were right on schedule, right down to the length of the ash on my cigar that I smoked as I stood beside her.

We got onto the stout-engined boat that plied the waters above the Falls and surged out to a small island. There, protected from the current and in view of the onshore crowd, Taylor entered the barrel. I supervised, that is, I helped her get settled, although she could do it all by herself. She was doing it herself, for although she entrusted herself to me in the wheelbarrow on the wire, this ride she was taking alone.

The lid was seated and sealed. There would be plenty of air in the barrel for as long as Taylor would be in it, but nevertheless we had set a rubber tube in the top that went down to her face for her to breathe through if necessary.

I pushed the tube aside just before they were ready to put the barrel into the water. "Taylor?" I said.

"I'm fine," she replied.

I nodded to the men, they hoisted and swiveled the derrick and lowered the barrel gently into the water behind the boat. We then drove out into the Canadian current, at more speed than I would have liked, but it was necessary to keep control in those strong waters.

The barrel was released just after four o'clock in the afternoon, about a mile above the lip of the Falls. There was no reason to stay. The water was high and there was little chance of the barrel getting hung up—or at least not before it got beyond the point where there was no possibility of our retrieving it. The boat set out at top speed for the dock.

I watched with the crowd. The barrel bobbed smartly upright, the 100-pound anvil in its base keeping it stable. It spun slowly in the current. So far, Taylor had not been tumbled end over end, and that was what I feared.

The barrel was visible to the crowd for the entire twenty minutes it took to reach the edge of the Falls, except while it passed through some of the upper rapids, where it was obscured by the height of the waves. They said that at the edge it tipped forward slightly and then was gone, presumably falling straight down over the Horseshoe Cataract of Niagara Falls.

I did not see this for I was with our manager, racing in his carriage to reach the dock of the Maid of the Mist on the lower river, where we would retrieve Taylor and the barrel.

The rocking boat and now the rocking carriage. Thank God our manager was uncharacteristically silent. I closed my eyes.

Konrad and I had walked several times across the gaping mouth of the Gouffre de Padirac in the Dordogne of France.

This is an immense hole in the ground. The surrounding land is relatively flat, but suddenly there is a change in the way the sunlight strikes the air, there is a cool silence, a feeling of unease overcomes you, something extraordinary is ahead. And then, as though it had just appeared from another world, you become aware of this yawning abyss, an emptiness, its round opening there on the face of the earth going to depths your eyes cannot penetrate, right in front of you, where there ought to have been solid ground.

Konrad and I walked the wire across Padirac with green mist rising around us. A good show. That was all right, but that madman Martel, the famous cave explorer, was not satisfied to have us merely walk across the hole. No, he said that alone would be wrong. This really *was* the entrance to another world, a fabulous underworld that one entered by being lowered on the end of a rope. Martel insisted that we must go down. Konrad dismissed this demand out of hand, but I was young and as dauntless as any of Martel's crew, so I let myself be lowered into the pit.

I had scrambled on rocks in the mountains; exploring the cave was much the same. But what came back to me now as I closed my eyes in the carriage was the rocking on the waters of the underground river of Padirac, for Martel took me in a tiny boat through some rapids into the depths of the cave. As we were reaching the shore, he put out all our lights for the sport of it, so I could experience true darkness as I never had before.

The rocking of the boat, well, I do not need firm ground, the wire always moves. But the black! I had not known. I thrust my hands before my eyes and there was only black, like a solid thing. This blackness which was all there was. It was not seen, it was simply there. I was terrified. Always on the wire, in fog, at dusk, even at night, there is some light. I have always been able to see where I was on the wire. (Even when blindfolded, for that is just a trick; you can look down and see the wire quite well.) In the blackness of this cave I began to lose my balance and feared that I would fall.

Martel laughed and relighted the lamps. We looked at another chamber and then returned to be pulled up again on the end of a rope to the surface. Konrad looked at my muddy clothes in disgust and spat. I suppose that it is as well that a man who walks above the surface of the earth should have seen what lies below. Once was enough.

Taylor!!!

Taylor's eyes were squeezed tightly shut. She could feel the hardness of the oak boards of the barrel even through the padding. Inside, the sealed barrel was the blackness of a tomb. It surged and jerked, moving at what felt to be a tremendous speed. Surely Charon never ferried anyone across the River Styx so fast.

Twenty minutes! Twenty minutes to spin in those waters,

before going over Niagara Falls in hopes of coming out alive as no one ever had before.

The incessant noise! The roaring of the water and the increasing thunder of the Falls ahead were as solid as the blackness that filled the barrel.

Taylor in the blackness of her casket interminably spun with the current toward the edge of the Falls. Would it never be over? Then the barrel tipped forward, was driven straight down as though thrust by a piston, pushed by a million tons of water.

Taylor lost consciousness.

The barrel did not have to withstand the blow of hitting the surface below. The waters enclosing it parted the surface, plunged deep into the basin, dispelled their force in the depths of the standing water, slowed their motion and released the barrel, nudged it aside until out from under the falling mass it bobbed to the surface. Taylor came to consciousness in a shaking frenzy as the barrel vibrated with the frothing waves. The barrel was caught in an eddy. It was passed on to another, then back to the first eddy again, slowly spinning.

Taylor heard the muffled shouting of the men who had thrown a rope around her barrel and were drawing it to the shore, where it clunked sharply against a rock, jarring her body severely.

She had not noticed a thing but the motion as she rode and fell, but now she hurt all over. Her back ached terribly. She reached up to wipe her wet face and her hand came away sticky with blood.

The barrel was jerked up onto the shore. Taylor moaned. They pried off the top, but she was too weak to climb out. They knocked off one of the slats and pulled her out. She was said to have been confused in her talk, but she walked along the shore to a boat and was taken down to the dock of the *Maid of the Mist*. When I arrived she nodded at me and went on talking to reporters. They headlined her advice: DON'T TRY IT.

In the carriage again at last I took her hand, but it was limp. She leaned her head on my shoulder and closed her eyes.

"My back hurts bad, Gravie" she said.

I took her to my hotel room—it was the first time—and had a hot bath prepared.

"I don't know, Gravie," she said, as I helped her take off her clothes. "That tub looks very like a barrel and I don't know whether I want to get in the water so soon again."

I looked at her startled. A tired merriment had returned to her eyes. She laughed weakly and stepped into the tub.

After a few days, Taylor's aches and pains were gone, but her troubles had just begun. I had already noticed some beginning of it in the newspapers—about the cat—but did not realize then how people would turn against her.

Of course, I was abandoning her too. I was used to looking at things as they were, and that is just how I saw it. I felt guilty, but Taylor had served her purpose for me. I do not carry excess baggage.

Taylor, in any case, was riding a wave of euphoria. She thought she had proved herself and was bound now to make it on her own. Her first lecture was packed, and despite some catcalls from the audience, it went well enough. Our manager had retrieved the barrel and put it back together and it stood on the platform at her side.

Taylor always had been able to talk.

Her second lecture did not go so well. Some people had come to heckle. One man stood up and denounced her as a crazy woman. He was removed from the hall, but the audience was not kind.

That second night I did not go up on the stage. My presence might have helped, but what if someone shouted an obscene remark about Taylor and me? Taylor did have to make it on her own. I do not think I could have helped.

Also, it was all over for Taylor and me. She recovered from her ordeal in almost manic high spirits, and demanded the last few days before I left that we repeat some of the more acrobatic of our initial sexual exercises. "I really do wish we could have done it on the wire, Gravie," she said.

She was quite serious. I know I was when I said I regretted it, too. I never have done it on the wire. I think maybe it was not meant to be done there.

That was all. My gear was shipped. Taylor and our manager— *her* manager, thank God no longer mine—saw me off on the ship from New York City. Taylor, a large woman waving from the dock in a brightly colored dress—I could see her for a long time—and then not again for twenty years.

I returned to Europe, to France, to the acclaim I so well deserved. The conquerer of Niagara Falls! Yes, they had heard about Taylor in her barrel, but that was an American stunt by an unknown lunatic, and a woman besides. I, on the other hand, had skillfully walked over the Falls (no one ever questioned the exact placement of the wire). The mayors and city councils of Europe all clamored to have me demonstrate my art. There are other wire walkers, of course, but there is only one Gravelet.

I walk the bouncing wire and my passages are visions, shimmering for a moment in the heavens, then gone, taken down, moved away, like the wire itself. Yet of those who have seen me against the sky, high, high above the ground, not one will ever forget. My performance is as light as the air itself, but its impact is that of solid stone. That is how it has been for thirty years, since Konrad died. It will not change. Moreover, after I am gone, they will say, "You see that church steeple there? And the clock tower across the way? I remember the time when Gravelet . . ."

We will all die. I will walk above the earth no more, and no one living will have ever seen me. Never mind. The legend will grow. Then I will be larger than life. No one will ever be able to compete with me. I will loom in the past as the giant no mere living mortal could ever hope to best. I know my business.

You say if I do not quit, one day I will walk the wire and find myself walking the plank, and step off. So be it. I will walk the wire while I live.

Mon Dieu! Why these morbid thoughts? I am only sixty. Konrad was in fine shape at seventy and would have walked another ten years if he had not been so set in his ways. The last time I carried anyone on *my* back was on my fiftieth birthday, and *she* was as light as a feather. I know how to take it easy.

Taylor did not write to me. She did send a postcard. Rather, it came with a packet of clippings and a final bill from my manager. For the rope.

The postcard was a picture of Taylor in her outfit standing beside her barrel. On the back she had written:

> For Gravie
> With Love,
> Annie

It was undated. I had never called her Annie.

The postcard was in my effects for a few years, and then I lost it somewhere. I never keep mementos. I used to keep clippings for promotion, but not for many years. There are collectors, you know, who keep scrapbooks about me. I *love* to look through them. I keep no scrapbook myself. I prefer memory to documents.

I did keep one clipping. It is yellow and brittle now. Someone sent it to me. There was nothing else in the envelope, which was addressed merely "The Great Gravelet, Paris, France," which was quite enough, and there was no return address. Do I think Taylor sent it? No. It was someone who meant to be mean.

It is a typical *New York Times* report of the day. A few city fellows took the train to Buffalo to view the Exposition, and while they were there they went to a lecture by Mrs. Anna Edson Taylor, billed as "The Conquerer of Niagara Falls." It reads like this:

> We entered the hall late to find that the lecture was not very well attended. A large oak barrel stood on the stage, and no more had we seated ourselves when a small hawker of a man who looked more like a pickpocket or a seller of sweat cloths than an entrepreneur came out onto the stage and began telling us the height of Niagara Falls and details about the barrel. "Bring on Mrs. Taylor," someone shouted, and there was an appreciative response from the audience to this request. No sooner said than done, the hawker turned and said, "Mrs. Taylor."
>
> Mrs. Taylor then navigated out onto the stage, I can use no other term, for she was a very large woman. I will say that she was dressed in the latest New York fashion. She waited for the rowdy applause to stop (even our crowd had taken a nip or two during the day), and then started her prepared monologue. I suppose she speaks well, but she was not addressing a female literary circle, and her style

was overdone by far, the foolhardy stunt itself being too crazy for drama. One certainly could shudder at the thought of being cooped up in that dark barrel rushing down the rapids to the edge of the Falls, but on the other hand, who but a lunatic would be in such a plight?

There was some laughter and then a well-turned-out gentleman stood up down in front, pointed to the stage, and looking back at the audience said in a deep booming voice, "Which one's the barrel?"

His auditors, particularly those among us looking for entertainment more than for edification, exploded in paroxysms of laughter. Many more and much ruder things were shouted.

Mrs. Taylor stood as though stunned until her manager, the little man, stole apologetically out onto the stage and led her away.

I was glad he did because although I appreciated the wit, Mrs. Taylor's stricken face was beginning to make me feel uncomfortable. Even so, what business did she have of making such a spectacle of herself? What she did was insane. This certainly was recognized by the New York State legislature in passing a bill last month expressly forbidding the use of Niagara Falls for stunts such as "Ships of Fools," idiots in barrels, Sam Patch divers, high-wire walkers, and other daredevils. If we can get the Canadians now to agree to establish an International Park surrounding the Falls, we can protect it from the desecration of benighted fools the likes of Mrs. Taylor.

I still grate at the inclusion of high-wire walkers in that list. I am *not* a daredevil, nor a fool.

Taylor's plight pained me, but as I have remarked, I was not wholly surprised at the turn of events. I wondered what she would do now. There was nothing I could do. We inhabited different worlds. I have kept that clipping in my wallet all these years, reading it whenever misanthropy overcame me at the stupidity of human affairs and I became disaffected with the world.

Botticelli's Venus rose out of the sea on a cockleshell. My Taylor was born from a barrel in the gorge below Niagara Falls.

Taylor . . . what *were* you doing in that barrel?

Here is how I came to see Taylor again. It was because of my investments. Oh, yes, after the Great War I looked again to America. I had begun investing as a hobby and in fact guessed right about America, for I bought property and am secure now despite the collapse of the stock market in 1929.

In 1921, I was in New York City pursuing my hobby. Also, I thought the New York City officials would be interested in having me walk across Times Square. Americans! It was as bad as Niagara Falls. I never did understand why the "Times Square Stunt" was forbidden—God knows the 1920s in America were filled with enough other stunts—but my lack of comprehension is partly because I soon ceased to make any effort to understand. I did walks in Toronto and Montreal and let New York City go to hell.

To get to Taylor. There was now no possibility whatsoever of walking across Niagara Falls itself. I could have repeated my walks across the gorge, but I saw no reason to do that, and any sentimental inclinations I might have had toward such a project were quickly flattened by the arguments and pleas of my old manager.

"Taylor?" he said. "Taylor? Oh, her. I don't know anything about her. She's probably dead by now."

I did not pursue the topic of Taylor.

I went on my own to view the Falls. At that time I was much taken by English tailoring and was impeccably suited. I wore a bowler hat and carried a furled umbrella. It was early

October, the weather was turning cold, there was a wind. Even had it started to rain from the overcast skies I would not have dared to open my umbrella as the wind might have lifted me right out over the Falls. I am still an admiring reader of Edgar Allan Poe. With all those signs, I should have turned back.

I dawdled, becoming absorbed in the noise and the mesmerizing sight of the slick gray water rolling over the edge of the Falls like cold molten steel.

I had noticed a pile of rags at the side of an unoccupied newspaper kiosk. No, that is not right. I had barely noticed . . . but did I even see anything at all? I may not have. Rich and well-dressed men learn not to see flotsam. It is likely to disturb one's peace of mind.

Suddenly a hand thrust out. "Buy a postcard, mister?"

The bundle struggled to its feet, and now I saw that there was indeed a pile of rags on the walkway, a carpetbag, a blanket, some old newspapers—in short, the worldly goods of this derelict who now placed in my protesting hand a postcard.

In reaching to give it back—I never buy from hawkers or give to beggars—I glanced at it and stopped, frozen. It was of a man on a wire, with a wheelbarrow . . .

I looked sharply at the woman, for I had been aware that it was a woman.

"Buy a postcard, mister?" she repeated when she saw my interest. "Five cents, six for two bits. I got lots." She quickly rummaged in the carpetbag and brought out some pictures of a large woman standing beside a barrel.

Taylor? Stooped, ancient, thin-faced, nothing like that big jolly woman I had known. But something about her . . .

I was terrified! *"Non! Non!"* I said, and tried to hand the postcard back to her. She would not take it, and as I let it go the wind whipped it out over the Falls. I watched it flutter, then turned to see Taylor looking at me. She was smiling and her eyes met mine.

In panic I tore a bill from my wallet—I do not know what denomination—and pressed it into her outstretched hand. She did not look at it, and it too was taken by the wind and sailed high into the air, out and over the Falls.

"Mister . . . ?" she said, a tone of uncertainty in her voice, a puzzled look in her eyes.

I could not stand it. Did she recognize me? I turned abruptly and walked off.

"Mister? Buy a postcard?"

It was a firm, loud, flat voice that came after me. Then her laugh. I did not hesitate another moment. I ran. I did not look back.

What was I to do? I was sure for a moment that she had recognized me. A crazy old woman selling postcards beside Niagara Falls.

Was it Taylor? I could have asked our old manager, but I did not want to know. I ran. It is the only cowardly thing I have ever done in my life. The *only* cowardly thing. Once is enough, though, is it not?

That old woman was emaciated. She was starving to death. You could see that. She was not clean. Her clothing . . . She certainly was not warm, crouched there beside a kiosk for dubious protection from the wind. Could she make any money at all selling postcards? I suppose in the summer some people would buy. There are always those who give pennies to beggars, as though that absolved them of blame.

I put the incident out of my mind. Not bloody likely, as the British say.

You know how memory can be. It was as though I had photographed the scene. It was Taylor all right. That wide grin, those eyes, the round set of the face. The laugh. I have never forgotten that laugh.

Taylor.

I have brooded on it these ten years. She was sixty-five then, and looked ninety. She would be seventy-five now, if she were still alive, which surely she is not, could not be, could not have survived another ten years in that condition, without enough to eat, with no place to stay.

Taylor.

I do not ask forgiveness, Taylor. I know I am a coward. There is nothing else I could do. I ran. I would run again, today.

Go on, say it. Say it in that flat Western voice, the tone that hints of sarcasm but is so neutral in its ambiguity that I never knew, never will know, what you really thought, Taylor. Go on. Say it.

"The *Great* Gravelet."

OVER THE FALLS

Remember me when I am gone away,
—Christina Georgina Rossetti

HEN I WAS A LITTLE GIRL, I HAD A petition:

June 21, 1866.
Hardy, Nebraska.
Please do not fire Mr. Hurd.

It was signed by all twelve pupils in our one-room school.

"Georgie Smith can't write," my mother said, glancing at the petition but not taking it. I presented it to her because she was the main one who got Mr. Hurd fired. It was too late, I knew that. He'd already left town by the time we children heard about it.

"I signed Georgie's name for him," I said.

My mother set the iron she'd been using on the flat top of the kitchen stove and picked up a hot one. I twisted up my petition.

"But *why* don't you like Mr. Hurd?" I asked her.

"He's a dipsomaniac!" she snapped, her voice rising to that pitch I knew as a warning signal. If I went on too long with her in that state she'd whop me with the yardstick. But I was roused, too.

"He's *not* a maniac," I said indignantly. "He's never whipped anybody."

"Look it up," my mother said triumphantly, arching her eyebrows. "Go on, look it up." Her greatest sacrifice to my education had been the purchase of a Webster's dictionary.

I bowed my head. She always got me when it came to the dictionary. Not that I didn't like the book, I loved it, really, and it was fun to just open it to see what words meant. So I was half over my anger by the time I found the word and muttered to myself, "We know that, dummy," when it said that a dipsomaniac was "One affected with dipsomania," which in turn means "A morbid and uncontrollable craving (often periodic) for drink, esp. alcoholic liquors; also, improperly, acute and chronic alcoholism." Next, I looked up *morbid.* "Not sound and healthful; induced by, or characteristic of, a diseased or abnormal condition; hence, abnormally susceptible to or characterized by emotional impressions, esp. of a gloomy or unwholesome nature." Then I looked up *acute, chronic* and *alcoholism.* That was enough. You could go on for hours looking up one word after another until you forgot what you started out with.

Of course Mr. Hurd drank. He had a bottle in his desk, and he took half-hidden sips throughout the day. You could smell his whiskey breath.

"He is not morbid," I returned to my mother. "He *likes* to drink, and he smiles. Besides, you misused the word. *Dipsomaniac* does not mean alcoholic," I said triumphantly.

My mother cocked her eyebrow at me and waited until I'd run down. "Drunkard," she said. "How about that? Look that one up if you like." She turned sharply back to her ironing.

He wasn't that, either, I thought, nothing like the mad, foul, angry, filthy, wife-beating drunks more than one of us schoolchildren knew about right in our own homes. It was unfair of my mother, because my own daddy was like that once a month. Between binges he was as teetotaling and anti-saloon as my mother. When I got older I argued with her and was disgusted at how she always accepted his conversion every time, month after month, year after year. But I guess she had her reasons. Daddy was all right if you stayed out of his way when he was "sick."

I sighed. Actually, I was bored in school because Mr. Hurd did not teach much. I would not really miss old Turd Hurd.

I could read. My mother taught me that. Any self-respecting mother would be ashamed to start a child to school who could not read. I knew how to add and subtract, divide and multiply, and I had a good round handwriting that hasn't changed to this day. I once memorized the multiplication tables up to twenty because there wasn't much else to do.

I liked reading best, and by the time I was ten I had read every book I could lay my hands on in that small town. "Hardy, Nebraska, population fifty-four," my daddy said, "not counting dogs but including snakes in the grass?

I knew all fifty-four people, so how could it include snakes in the grass?"

"But it should include dogs too," I argued when I figured it out. Certainly I felt like a dog on more than one occasion myself.

Our new teacher was an old spinster. Why, she must have been at least forty! We children thought she was ancient, but I'd sure be happy to be that age again myself, a woman in her prime. Mr. Hurd could not discipline himself, let alone us, but Miss Fahrquardt was certainly in control. "Fart Cart," we called her. I soon felt guilty doing it. You don't snicker at someone who changes your life.

As I say, I could read, and had read everything I could find, including the Bible.

"But she shouldn't read . . ." my mother said to my daddy.

"What?" he teased her.

"Well, the Song of Solomon, for one thing," she said, her face angry and embarrassed at the same time.

"And why not?" he guffawed.

Boy, did I race to read the Song of Solomon!

"But it's beautiful, Mama. Why shouldn't I read it?"

My mother wasn't talking. And it was years before I understood my father's amusement. How amazing it is that those verses could mean so much to me as a child, and then so much more as a young woman, when the layers of meaning showed through, then as a wife and mother. They don't mean so much now that I'm an old woman, I admit. I was never all that religious anyway, and now I go to church mostly for warmth and a place to sit down.

Of course the Bible was mine to read. I was, after all, a Sunday school girl, raised to trust in Jesus (not that I put much stock in the Lord's help—prayer had never done me a particle of good that I could see).

Do you suppose it's really true, all that stuff about heaven and hell? It's not in the Bible, you know, not the way the preachers tell it. But like I said, there are layers of meaning there that I suppose will be revealed in due time, maybe. I've never been frantic about death and dying like some people, moaning and groaning. Why, they make so much noise in some of those churches you can't even sleep (that's a joke).

And that's just what I wanted to get to here, about what's packed inside ordinary sentences. One day Miss Fahrquardt went to the blackboard and said she was going to show us what a sentence was, and she wrote one down. I turned around and smirked, because I sure knew what a sentence was. But then she proceeded to peel that sentence apart like an onion, opened it out like an orange, to reveal the insides of such simple sentences as *The tree is in the yard*, or *My dog's name is Spot*.

I was amazed. It had never occured to me that a sentence had parts. Even the sentences we use in ordinary speech are deep and full. I couldn't get enough of it, and as I say, it changed my life.

I want to get on with the story of my life, but first I have to make sure you understand about sentences. Yes, I know about that Frenchman who learned one day that he had been speaking prose all his life. But don't you see? All he learned was a new name for his talk. There weren't any new worlds opening out for him as there were for me when Miss Fahrquardt began outlining sentences on the board and explained the different parts and how they fit together. When she unpacked those sentences I felt faint, truly I did, because I never knew that there was so much *inside* a sentence that you can't ordinarily see. I didn't think of it then, but when I was older I realized that sentences are like pregnant women. They're full of hidden things, you never know quite what. Because even the simplest sentence can have different meanings.

I knew about puns, words spelled the same that mean different things, words spelled differently that sound the same, smutty words enclosed in longer proper words. But how hidden and mysterious everything is never came home to me so much as it did when Miss Fahrquardt took sentences and showed that they aren't just open expressions of what one has to say, but instead are wrapped packages ready to surprise.

I loved surprises. And I had never known the like before. Do you think this was silly of me? And that I'm a silly old woman to make so much of it now? Please, I beg of you, try to be that ten-year-old girl. Think how flat Nebraska is, both in landscape and in speech. There's this child reading, in love with words and books. A rather snotty self-satisfied prig of a little girl, who in the department of reading thought herself to be quite as good or even better than her teacher, Mr. Hurd, thank you very much, an old man of twenty-nine or thirty. Little Miss Know-It-All, how she did preen!

Then here comes this woman, as old as her grandmother almost, this pinch-mouthed spinster teacher, Miss Fahrquardt, would you believe? One morning she wrote a sentence on the blackboard and showed me things could be more than what they seem. When I turned back from my smirk, she had drawn neat slanted lines and laid that sentence open like a butchered hog. Even before I understood, I realized something wonderful had happened, and I truly had to gasp for breath.

Later when Miss Fahrquardt gave me Shakespeare to read, I was ready for the sentence *There are more things in heaven and earth, Horatio, than are dreamt of in your philosophy.*

Now I've been so earnest about sentences that I've come all over shy, an old woman in her second childhood. Come off it—was it really like that? Yes, I think it was, something like. I loved old Miss Fahrquardt, and there was nothing grander I could think to do than prepare to be a teacher just like her. Six years later I took the examinations and got certified and went out to take a school on my own.

Just sweet sixteen! But I was a full-grown woman nonetheless, and sure of myself, I tell you!

The story of my life. I was a big ugly girl. It never bothered me much because I could take care of myself and never thought there was anything I couldn't do. I remember the time I beat up that big bully Georgie Smith. I got astraddle him and both hands in his hair and was thumping his head on the ground when Miss Fahrquardt grabbed me by the shoulders. It would have taken some doing to pull me off, but I let go and got up. My stockings had pulled down and I had bloody knees, but I paid them no mind. Georgie Smith never bothered my little brother again, nor anybody else while I was around.

Miss Fahrquardt punished me by making me carry buckets of coal for the school stove, but it was a pleasure. I was strong and willing. I pumped water and helped my mother with the washing she took in. I hoed the garden, cooked, took care of the younger children. And I put boys in their place.

Not that I didn't like boys, I liked them a lot. And I knew I could get as much attention by helping them with their homework as fancy Jeanne Simmons did with her pretty face. I put everything into my strength and never worried about my looks or that I would be an old maid. It's funny, even though I was preparing to follow in the footsteps of an old spinster schoolteacher, I knew I would find a husband.

Matthew Taylor was just what I thought I'd get. He was not a very practical man, weaker than me in many ways, and needing me to take care of him. He was far from weak in other ways, though. He was from Omaha, and had gone to college there and made himself a lawyer. But he wasn't sharp enough for city law, so he came out and set up in Superior, to be circuit lawyer for wheat farmers and ranchers and the people of Nuckolls County, Nebraska. A hard life for a weak man, you say? That it was, for Matthew was not only soft on people's troubles and could never face them down to get his fees, he was also physically weak. I could tell all that when I first saw him, and knew he needed me and that we would get along just fine.

Superior was a bigger town than Hardy, where I'd grown up. There were over 200 people in Superior, and I'd been teaching there already four years. Matthew came to the box social at the start of the school year. All the girls and women brought a supper for two people in a box fancied up with ribbons and bows and they were sold to the highest bidders among the men and boys. It was supposed to be a secret, but they always knew whose box was being bid on, and they tried to get the one they wanted to sit and eat with. The young folk set a lot of store on it and sometimes there were fights. The money went for school supplies, and we sure needed it.

I knew all about Matthew Taylor. He'd been in Superior for a whole month, after all. We'd already met eating dinner at folks' houses, because you'd better believe there were matchmakers in Superior and they'd just about despaired of getting me married off. He may have wondered at the time how I looked at him because I already knew he was mine.

So when he came into the school where all the desks and benches had been pushed back against the wall, I steered him to the middle of the room to the table with all the box suppers on it. I put my hand on my box supper and whispered, "Matthew, buy this one."

"What?" he asked.

"This one," I said, nodding at him with a big smile.

"Yes, all right," he said, sort of worried.

Then I let him go over and talk with the men.

He bought it, but it cost him a pretty penny. Two of the first-grade boys had saved their pennies all summer to bid on my box. So when it was held up, before anyone else could say a word, Jimmy Andersen said loud and clear, "I bid a penny."

Everybody laughed, because most bids started out at a nickel. Jimmy turned red, but he stood his ground. And before the laughing was over, Benny Dondlinger said, "I bid two pennies."

The boys glared at each other. A hush came over the room, and some little girls started to titter. But some of the men frowned severely, which was pretty difficult for them to do when they were so amused. Jimmy and Benny didn't see anybody but each other and that box. It was a nice box. I'd fixed it up real pretty, with dry thistle heads for decoration, which some of the women complimented me on.

"Shush, shush," several people said.

"Three," Jimmy said.

Then Art Palmer, who always was the auctioneer at local sales and was presiding now, spoke up firmly and said, "I'm-a-bid-a-three, a three, for-this-a-nice-a-box," he held it up. "Do I hear a four? Need a four."

"Four," Benny said.

"And a five," Art said, "for the box, come on five, have a four, need a five, who's got a nickel for the very fine box?"

"Five!" Jimmy said, and jingled his pennies loudly in his pocket.

"Whoop—oh!" one of the men yelled, and picked Jimmy up and set him out in the middle of the room. Another man stood Benny facing Jimmy and then stepped back.

"Six," Benny said.

Art carried on with his auctioneer's talk, longer and longer each time, running it out. "Do I hear ten cents? I do! Ten cents! A big fat *silver* dime!"

As the bidding moved on and reached twenty cents, I looked sadly over at Matthew. He had been set to start the bidding at a nickel as he'd seen others do, but he hadn't had a chance. He stood there with his mouth open, and gave me a frantic look. I shrugged at him with a smile.

"Twenty cents! Two dimes! Would you believe it? Not that it ain't worth every penny of it, this very fine box, but who'd have ever thought that this little tyke would have saved up so much money? By God, if this ain't a great bid and a great auction!"

Several of the men whooped again.

"Twenty-one," Jimmy said when everyone quieted down.

Benny looked worried and Art's voice became softer. Everybody knew the end was in sight.

"Twenty-two."

"Twenty-three."

"Twenty-four," Benny said with terror in his eyes.

And before Art could get in with another line of patter, Jimmy shrieked "Twenty-five!" and Benny burst out in tears.

People cheered and some of them tried to calm Benny down, who was sobbing. When the hollering quieted down I glanced over at Matthew and could see he didn't know what to do. This was the first box social he'd ever been to, and before I could stop him he cleared his throat—everybody turned toward him—and he blushed just like Jimmy had who'd started the bidding.

"Twenty-six," he said, and now Jimmy burst out bawling.

It was pandemonium.

"Shame!" somebody shouted, and there was booing.

Then above the uproar Art Palmer shouted, "Time out!"

Everybody quieted down again. Benny and Jimmy were taken aside by several men, who crouched down and got out their handerkerchiefs to dry the boys' tears and, glancing back over their shoulders at Matthew, talked to them. Pretty soon the men stepped back and the two boys stood together, smiles on their tear-streaked faces.

"Come on Art, let's get on with the auction," one of the men said.

"'Deed, oh," Art said. "I got a twenty-six. Is there another bid?"

"Twenty-seven," Jimmy said.

Matthew looked around, mortified that he'd done something wrong, until one of the men said gruffly, "Well, you gonna bid or ain't you?"

"Twenty-eight," Matthew said.

Thank goodness, he had enough sense not to bid more than a penny at a time. People cheered up again, and there was clapping and laughter as the bidding increased until finally Jimmy said, "Forty-nine," which everybody knew was all the money the two boys had in combination.

"I got forty-nine," Art raised his voice and carried on for several minutes at a fast rate until everyone was stomping and yelling. Finally Art shouted, "Do I hear fifty?"

The noise stopped and everyone looked at Matthew.

Matthew had his handerkerchief out and he mopped the sweat off his brow. He looked around and cleared his throat. "Fifty," he said, his voice cracking.

Everybody cheered and the men who had sworn at Matthew earlier now clapped him on the back. Jimmy and Benny jumped up and down, because they knew as well as anybody that the bidding never went over two-bits, twenty-five cents, and that nobody, but nobody, had ever paid as high as fifty cents for a box before.

I was just as happy as could be, because everybody knew it was my box. I whispered to Jimmy and Benny that I'd read to them at the noon hour on Monday, and they ran off whooping. Then I went over and took Matthew's arm and everybody cheered and we were as good as married right then and there. Matthew looked proud and bewildered. He'd done the right thing after all. He coughed from men whopping him on the back, but he stood it well and smiled at me. Fifty cents was more than he could actually afford to spend.

I felt a little sorry for Matthew, but not all that much. I mean he was a fair-looking man, not handsome, but maybe he'd rather have had a smaller woman for a wife, someone more his own size, and pretty. I suppose he might have gotten a prettier woman, but I doubt if he'd ever have had the gumption to try. Not that he didn't like a woman and all that. Oh no! He had no problems there like some men do, and I liked the woman's duty well enough. Truth to say, I doted on it, and he sure never had any complaints along that line no matter how much comforting he wanted. And he needed a lot, right up to the end. They say that sort of heating up comes from having TB.

We got married that winter. I was twenty and Matthew was twenty-four. Right after the wedding he took sick to bed, which didn't bother me at the time because I knew he had a weakly constitution and I'd have to look after him.

"Since you're in bed anyway," I said to my sick new husband, which was the best way I had of caring for him.

"I don't suppose I'm so sick I wouldn't like company," he'd say.

So not much more than nine months later I had Jane. But I

kept right on teaching. She was such a good baby. I took her along with me and she slept in a crib by the school stove. All the children helped take care of her. But then less than a year later Teddy came, and he was colicky. I had to hold and rock him, but nothing would stop his yelling. Jane was still a baby and there were diapers to wash, and the upshot was that I had to give up teaching even if we couldn't afford to lose the money.

"What's *that?*" Matthew asked.

"You're not supposed to know about it," I said.

"But I can feel it."

I cuddled him and said, "You don't want any more babies, do you?"

"If we could afford them . . ." He was genuinely distressed, because he truly did like children.

Anyway, the pessary worked because I didn't have any more children. I'd have been willing to have a dozen, and could have, I was built for it. Having a baby just made me bigger and stronger. But we couldn't afford it. We scraped along and I did some work for some of the women in town, taking in washing and doing housecleaning, like my mother had.

Then when the children were five and six, Matthew rode in late one evening at the beginning of winter. There had been a feathering of snow and the moon was bright, a sharp cold pretty night. I could hear him coughing putting the horse in the shed, even through the closed doors and windows of the house. So I had the hot water and warm clothes ready, and honey to put in the strong bark tea.

"Matthew!" I was so shocked I almost didn't know what to do, and was plenty glad the children were in bed. His handkerchief was frozen bright red against his face with blood, and though he kept nodding to me that he was all right, he was coughing and choking and spitting up blood. He slumped down on a kitchen chair and just let me take over. I pulled off his boots and his clothes and put my man to bed, and he never really got up proper again though it took him six months and buckets of blood to die.

" . . . Sorry," he said as I tucked him in.

"Shush," I said, and bustled about to take his mind off it, and mine too. He managed to drink some tea and settled down, not so much in sleep as in exhaustion.

The next day I moved our bed into the kitchen in front of the cookstove. It was the biggest room in the house, and the only warm one. We spent most of our time there anyway.

Dying is a funny thing. It wasn't an easy time for us, yet looking back I can see it was a good time. Matthew was weak as a kitten, but often his spirits were high. I'd come home with washing and see the two children pulled up to his bed on a chair.

"In the shed," Matthew said.

"Yes," Jane giggled, "but you can't see me."

"What about me? What about me?" Teddy butted in.

"You later," Matthew said. "I've got to find Jane first. Behind the stanchion."

"Nope," Jane wiggled in delight.

"Under the feed box."

"Nope."

"Behind the door."

"Nope."

"But there isn't anyplace else you could hide," Matthew said in exasperation. "You're cheating."

"I am not!" Jane said indignantly. "You just don't want to admit you can't find me."

"I give up," Matthew said.

"I'm up on the roof rafters!" Jane shrieked with laughter.

"Now me, now me," Teddy said. "See if you can find me."

Matthew couldn't read to the children, his voice wasn't up to it, so he had them read to him, and they adored doing it. He would whisper instructions and they were his arms and legs. They cleaned the house and even did the cooking.

I was sure proud of all of them.

It was a good thing they took to it so well, because I had to go out and scratch for a living. Matthew helped me go through his books, and then I rode around trying to collect back fees and to gather in what work Matthew could still do at home. Some people were good about it, paying up and even making up some things Matthew could do. But more than a few saw profit in our trouble. It was as though because Matthew was dying they didn't have to pay any debts to him. They just waited for him to die. Others wouldn't give him even the little jobs they knew perfectly well he could do, seeming not to want to have anything to do with a dying man, or even to know about it. I was in a high state of dudgeon the first few weeks, but I got over it. People are the way they are. I was thankful to those who helped.

When I'd ridden around and collected all I was going to get, I sold the horse. Even the children who loved that mare understood, or maybe they were afraid to object for fear that they would hear what they didn't want to know. We'd already given notice on Matthew's main street office because even though it was hard and callous in what it meant—that he would never go back there again, never work again—and it hurt, we simply couldn't afford to waste even those few dollars rent. Mr. Sykes, who owned that building, was one of the mean ones, and though we gave a month's notice on the 12th, he said we had to pay to the end of that month, and then another full month besides. Not very likely! Right then and there I counted out just what the rent was up to the 12th, and then exactly one month's rent after that, shoved it across his desk to him, and walked out. Well, lots of folks brought us food and helped us, which was good, but it's the mean things you remember longest.

I guess what being poor is is having to remember the mean things. It's not having the money or security to maintain illusions such as pretending that Matthew was going to live and not die.

"I picked you out," I said to Matthew, lying in bed with him late at night, cozy in the red flicker of the fire in the cooking stove.

"I know," he said.

"You're not mad at me because I did?"

"No, I'm glad." He paused a long while. "But it hasn't worked out so well for you."

"Shush," I said. "It's all right."

I wasn't sorry, but I guess I felt, oh, not cheated, but a little unhappy about it. It isn't exactly that I picked Matthew cold like, though it could have been somebody else. What I mean is that when it was time for me to marry—and it was high time—any man of his type would have done. But it happened to be Matthew, my Matthew, and I loved him. He was the father of my children and he treated them and me so good. He treated me so much better than my own daddy treated my mother that it made me sad to think about it. Though what can I know about how they got on in bed, where it all comes out? She certainly never told me!

Most of all, Matthew loved me.

"I love you," I said.

He just nodded his head.

"I really do."

"You're telling me?" He looked at me in that shy laughing way he had. "Why, you had me in bed very nearly before we got the door closed behind us after the wedding."

"You better believe it," I said, cuddling him.

"Annie," he said, all sober now. "You really were a lot for me to take in. I didn't know what was happening. I admit I was uneasy about it, but everything went so fast, and we were married, and you were pregnant, and it was all over." He thought a while. "Then Jane came," he smiled, "and I knew it was all right."

Toward the end he said, "It's peculiar. I find myself a contented man. I love my family, and I've never been happier in my life than these last few months. Isn't that strange?" he said, turning to me.

I couldn't say anything.

He loved me. He really did. I snuffled back my tears. It was really true.

Well, that's what he said, but he didn't need to. I knew it. We talked away those long winter nights before he died that spring. And loved. His desires seemed to go up with his fever, and I was always good to him. He was a dying man, my own, I loved him, and who was to say that this or that was better than hugging him in bed? I was extra careful, though, for it would be enough for a widow to raise two children without bringing from Matthew's deathbed into the world a third.

Because I knew I wouldn't find another man, or not one who would be all right.

"But you like men, Annie," Matthew said in a sort of desperation. "You like a man in bed and you're good for a man. Now, I *order* you. When ... when ... You get married again, you hear me? Annie?"

"Sure, sure," I said, and smoothed his brow.

"I order you, Annie! Now you get married."

"I'd say pretty much I already am," I laughed.

The wonder of it was how much we laughed. Sometimes the children would hear us at night and wake up and come to snuggle in bed with us.

God, how strange.

Sure there were other men who would have me. Matthew hadn't been buried two weeks when Charlie Combs pulled up in front of the house with his team and wagon.

"Annie, I need a wife," he said without preliminaries.

"You lack a heap more than that," I shot back at him.

"You're big and strong," he said, dribbling tobacco juice through his grizzled beard. "My last wife," he shook his head, "she didn't have no strength at all."

"Charlie Combs, you've worked two women to death already, and I don't intend to be the third." I turned around and went back into the house.

Charlie took out his plug and shaved another chew, and then he just sat there the whole rest of the afternoon. He came back the next day, and the next—in a new pair of overalls I noticed—and he sat there idle with that fine team not doing a lick of work.

Charlie Combs! I tell you, it was the most impressive courting Nuckolls County had ever seen. People came to watch him sitting there.

"Pr-e-tty . . . slow . . . action," I said to the children, sending them into shrieks of laughter.

People spoke to Charlie, and I nodded to him when I came and went, but he didn't want any small talk. This was serious business. It was spring planting time. He should be working, and for Charlie—and for his wife, I might add—that meant from three o'clock in the morning until eleven o'clock at night. Every day, every hour, every minute even, he sat there idle in front of my house . . . well, it was just unbelievable.

I went about my business and tried to ignore him, but I was weakening. People joked to me about it at first, but then they got sore at me. Charlie ought to get back to tending his affairs. "You shouldn't be keeping him from his planting," people told me.

"Me? Me keeping *him* from *his* work? Think how he's disturbing *my* work."

My work didn't amount to much. Charlie had one of the biggest farms around. Not only was I now wronging him in people's eyes, I was fast being viewed as a plumb fool. Charlie was a hard man and not easy on his wives, but I didn't have a husband, I had two children to raise, and I *was*, after all, big and strong.

Thank God for a thunderstorm. Not that Charlie sought shelter from it, not in the world. He sat there like it was a sunny summer day, getting soaked. But after the storm passed, he got to thinking.

"Goddamn!" he said finally. Or I reckon that's what he said, for I didn't hear him. I just happened to look out the front door an hour or so after the storm, and he was gone. The sun was already out warming the ground, and tomorrow would be the best day for planting that spring.

I can't actually say I waited him out, but as soon as I knew he was really gone and back at work, an enormous weight lifted off my back. Folks were good about it and soon got to laughing at Charlie's courting, but then they'd stop and shake their heads. I laughed a lot too, nervous like. It had been a close one.

And that was my main chance. My holding out against

Charlie discouraged a couple of others. And younger men could get younger, prettier wives, not so big as I was. And without two children already. Thank goodness Jane and Teddy were ready to go to school, because that was what saved us.

People gave us a lot of food at Matthew's funeral and I still took in washings and did housework, but that wasn't going to be enough because there isn't much work of that sort in a small town. Then in the middle of the summer the president of the school board came to see me and said they'd just fired the teacher.

"Never liked the fellow," he said.

I'd already heard this was going to happen, so I said, "Oh, he wasn't as bad as a teacher I had once."

"No? Well, doesn't matter now. We're all glad to have you back."

"Now that the children are old enough I was thinking about asking even before Matthew got sick," I said, to make us both understand it wasn't charity trumped up to fit my situation.

There wasn't much time for us to mourn, what with Charlie's courting, and getting ready for school again. Jane was ready for first grade and I started Teddy early, and it all worked out just fine. I moved the bed back into the bedroom, but it was a long time before we got used to being in the kitchen without Matthew.

So I kept those two children of mine right there in school for the next ten years until there were no more excuses in things I could teach them. Teddy, the younger one, worked a year on a ranch and I thought he was making his way all right when one day midweek he came in all clean and slicked up. And a bit of liquor on his breath, too, truth to tell.

"Why aren't you out working?" I asked.

He grinned and said, "Me and Joe Henderson are setting out for California."

I just sat down and looked at him. Ever since Matthew died there had been something for me to do, something to occupy my mind, but now suddenly it was a blank. An emptiness opened up before me, and it was like it had been there all the time, I'd just refused to look at it. My children were going to leave me, hadn't I known they would? There wasn't anything here for Teddy, not really. And Jane, well, I knew she was unhappy. She didn't want to teach school like her mom, and she hadn't found anything to do nor anybody she wanted to marry. Now she didn't say a word. She and I looked at each other, silent for a minute, and then I turned to Teddy and I said, "Jane's going, too."

"Hell's conniptions!" Teddy said, stomping on the floor, his hair getting mussed up as it always did when he got riled.

"Watch your tongue," I said. "You want to go, don't you, Jane?" I asked her.

Jane nodded.

"There's nothing here for Jane," I said, turning back to Teddy, who was sputtering.

"But ..."

"Goats butt."

"But me and Joe Henderson are going to work our way out there, probably have to walk on foot a lot, it'll be a hard trip. Jane can't do that," he said, all reasonable and hopeful like.

"I've saved some money," I said. "You can take it. It's enough to get you out there on the train. You might as well get right on out there, it'll be best for all of you."

"Joe Henderson ..."

"There's enough for him, too," I snapped.

"Look, Joe and I'll go on out, and then I'll send for Jane when we get settled."

"I don't want Jane traveling out there all alone by herself, do you?"

Teddy lowered his head. He knew when he was licked.

"But we're ready to go."

"You can stay with your old mom for another week," I said, a catch coming into my voice, and I turned away.

"Aw, mom," he said, coming over, the big little man of the house again. He put his arms around me, clumsy like. He hadn't hugged me since he was a little boy. I patted him on the shoulder.

"Well, you've all grown up," I said as brightly as I could, and stood up. "Now come on, we've got a lot to do to get you ready to go out into the world. Why, it seems like only yesterday when I left home."

I looked at them and was sad to see how excited they were. But glad, too, because I wouldn't have wanted them to cling. They were good children. I'd miss them. I'd be alone.

They stayed home another week and Jane and I sewed new clothes for her. Their friends had a going-away party for them, and then they took off and I didn't see them again for years, and that's a fact. I almost went to visit them while I was still in Superior, but I just couldn't get up the gumption to do it. Jane married someone else—not Joe Henderson, I mean, though that would have been all right. I sure wouldn't have sent them off together if I'd thought it wasn't! Teddy got a job in San Francisco.

Anyway, there I was alone again as I was twenty-two years before when I was just seventeen and had come to Superior to be the young schoolmarm, with my whole life before me. Now fall was coming again and I was the *old* schoolmarm, the Widow Taylor, whose children had flown the coop, and I was alone again.

The town liked me and the children liked me and I liked them. But nothing happened for the next five years. You know what I mean? The only thing I can recall is getting letters from Jane and thinking about going out to see my children in California, but I never did anything about it. I don't recall another thing other than just the same old thing, getting ready for school, teaching, being glad the school year was over, and then getting ready again.

One day I was reading a newspaper and I saw this advertisement:

> WANTED. Brave man to ride the rapids in a barrel through the Niagara Falls gorge. Make a name for yourself in the history books. Contact Harry Calicutt, Niagara Falls, New York.

I tore the advertisement out and pinned it on the kitchen wall, and after looking at it every day for a week, I sat down to write a letter:

> Dear Sir,
> I am a woman, but I am strong, and I . . .

I what? I could say I needed a job, but I didn't. That I was brave? Well, sure, I even rode steers in the town rodeo until I got so old I was embarrassed by it. Matthew encouraged it until he died. He took particular delight in my winning prizes. I could say that probably riding the rapids was something like riding steers, and I could do it.

What attracted me most about the advertisement I tried not to think of at first, but later I clung to it. I saw that Mr. Calicutt was right. If I were to do that thing, ride in that barrel, my name would go down in history books. I knew about Sam Patch and his name was at least in a geography book in the section on Niagara Falls. Sam Patch dived from the top of the Falls into the basin below. There wasn't much more than that said about him, and I didn't learn until later that he'd been killed trying it again. But that had been fifty years ago and nobody had done anything like it since. There was his name in the book. Sam Patch. I had a good name, too, but nobody knew it. Anna Edson Taylor. Why not put my name in a book?

Yes, by God, my life was empty and I wasn't going to do anything else. Why not ride in that man's barrel?

> Dear Sir,
> I am a woman, but I am strong. I have ridden steers in a rodeo. I am able and willing to ride a barrel through the rapids.
> Yours very truly,
> Anna Edson Taylor

There wasn't any reply to my letter, and in truth, I guess I hadn't really expected one. I more or less forgot all about it except the advertisement was still pinned on the kitchen wall when one day about six months later the stationmaster from the train depot came to my house to give me a telegram. He looked at me full of questions for of course he knew what it said:

> July 1, 1901. Anna Edson Taylor, Superior, Ne-braska. Job open. Come immediately. Harry Calicutt, Niagara Falls, New York.

I smiled and said thank you to the stationmaster, but not another word. I knew that within an hour everybody in town would know about my summons from Niagara Falls.

I sat down at the kitchen table with the telegram spread out in front of me. I took down the advertisement and smoothed it out, too. All I can remember is that I tried to figure out what some of the other advertisements were that had been torn in two when I ripped it out.

There was a timid little knock at the door. I knew who it was. I got up and folded the advertisement and the telegram and put them in my apron pocket. "Tillie Mae! What on earth are you doing knocking at my kitchen door? You half scared me to death."

"Why, I thought . . . I thought maybe I shouldn't just walk in on you with things on your mind."

"Me? With something on my mind? When did you ever know a woman with anything but an empty head?"

"Oh," Tillie Mae said in exasperation, "now you're teasing me."

"Why, I've never done that," I said.

But Tillie Mae was too excited to be baited. She sat down quickly at the table and said, "You got a telegram! From Niagara Falls."

"That I did," I said, taking it out, but leaving the advertisement in my pocket. Nevertheless, Tillie Mae darted her eyes around, and I know she saw that the advertisement was gone. I'd never talked about it to her, but I knew she'd read it.

"Mr. Calicutt is the president of the Niagara Falls school board," I said, handing Tillie Mae the telegram. "I'm going there to teach school."

"Oh?" Tillie Mae said, taking the telegram, and looking from it to me with doubt and disappointment in her eyes. "Is that so?"

"Yes. It's really quite an advancement for me. It's a bigger school and there's more money. But also with the children gone I do feel like I need a change."

"And leave all your old friends?"

"Well, there's that, too," I said.

Tillie Mae spread the word, and though there were leading questions, I stuck to my story. It was reasonable for me to take a better job.

Things really go fast once a turn is taken. I'd seen that before—marrying Matthew and having children, Matthew dying, and the children leaving home. I was glad it was summer, because I could never have gone if school had started. Now it was easy. Too easy when you stop to think about it. Even though I'd lived in Superior for nearly thirty years and raised my family there, I was still not a native. Hardy, where I'd come from, was only eight miles away, but it was on the Kansas border and had a reputation for saloons and drinking. There was no telling what things in my past might have been calling me away. People speculated, and a couple of awful stories got back to me. Now, why was that?

I don't say that there weren't some people who tried to talk me into staying. But even Tillie Mae, my best friend next door for ever since I'd lived in that house—who'd gone to school with me—even she didn't act as though there were any chance I'd change my mind.

Yes, I was stubborn, they all knew that. But you'd have thought they might have cared more. It was sobering to me, and taught me a lesson. It made me see I'd made the right choice. Because all my adult life was exposed to me there as amounting to not much. So I was glad enough to be going when I saw how everyone took it and how little my absence would really matter to the town.

They soon decided on a new teacher, and it was Tillie Mae! She didn't have a certificate, but they'd see to that later. And she had been born and raised in Superior, so was unlikely later to be called away by a mysterious telegram from the East.

Old Widow Taylor. That was me. Old Widow Taylor had

been schoolmarm in Superior for a long time and lots of people now grown up had gone to school to her and would remember her affectionately. I knew that, and always before it had satisfied me, but now it didn't. It wasn't enough. I tried not to think seriously about my name in history books, but I could think of little else because it was being brought home to me so firmly what it means to be not much of anybody. I understood now that it meant something to be somebody, that it meant something to me to be somebody. I saw that now I could be somebody, me who had never thought of being anybody before. That was why I was going and I wasn't a bit sorry to leave.

I had a sale. House, furniture, and everything, with Art Palmer the auctioneer just as he'd been years ago at the box social where I got Matthew. When it was over, all I had left fitted in two suitcases. I gave my books to the school. I did keep the Bible Matthew bought when we got married, with our few dates recorded in it. I've lost it since, but it doesn't matter. I remember.

They had a big going-away party for me, and old students of mine came from all over. They gave me a quilt with all their signatures on it, which a lot of women had worked on day and night to get ready on such short notice. It was nice, but it was something more to carry.

The schoolchildren saw me off on the train. That fall they wrote me a group letter, Tillie Mae saw to that. And she wrote me herself a few times, but I haven't heard any news from Superior now for a long time.

As soon as I got on the train, I called the conductor and said, "Please, would you go forward and buy six cigars for me? Get real good ones, now, because they're a special gift."

He came back with them and gave me my change, and I

tipped him a dime. We talked real friendly for a while, and then he went away and I locked myself in the ladies lounge and sat in the easy chair looking out the window at the Nebraska plains going by and smoked a cigar. Did it make me heady! We children had smoked when we were growing up, but I sure hadn't done it for a long time. Despite my getting dizzy, it tasted real good and I liked it a lot. And that's how I started smoking cigars.

How did I do it—leave my home? Or maybe you might ask how *could* I do it? I thought about it there smoking that cigar, and I've thought about it since. As Mr. Gravelet (I'll tell about him later), as Mr. Gravelet used to say, *"Pourquoi-pas?"* which is French and means in English, "Why not?"

I was forty-five years old, I was in the prime of my life in brains and fitness, and I would probably live to be a hundred if I stayed there in Superior, Nebraska. I could have gone on teaching school until kingdom come.

But I didn't see any point in doing that because I'd been a schoolteacher and a wife and a mother and it was all over and done with. Like Matthew, I'd already lived a life, except unlike him I wasn't dead. Oh, I know I was luckier than a lot of widows. I did have a job and could make my own way. I even owned that little house, having paid for it over the years. But somehow it wasn't enough. It just wasn't much. I wanted to do and be something more, not just the Widow Taylor, a schoolmarm growing old. Old Widow Taylor. That really got to me.

It isn't that I objected to growing old—that is, in due time. But not just yet. Why, I was strong as an ox and my spirits were as lively as when I was sixteen. It wasn't right for me to be Old Widow Taylor just yet. I can't say my discontent was deep, but it was as broad as my own beam, which had gotten pretty broad over the years.

Oh, I know I looked old and beyond doing anything more with my life than just teaching school. Even Charlie Combs had gotten himself a younger wife, who was bound, this time, to work *him* to death.

It was just that I looked out over all those years ahead thinking how long they were and how dumb it would be, in a way, to live them. It wasn't that I was so dissatisfied and unhappy, because I didn't worry about those things and I had friends. And if I gave out a lot to the children, they gave back a lot to me in the pride of their accomplishments. But it was always the same.

The stream of my life was so shallow and sluggish that there was hardly any flow. It wasn't worth a hill of beans, it seemed to me, to be moving so slowly and going nowhere. Sure, teaching is an honorable service to mankind. Then what?

Not out of discontent so much as from not caring did I sell and pack up and go to Niagara Falls. It just didn't matter. It might make my life better or worse, but whichever, it would be a change, and the difference would make me feel I was alive. That would be true even if I found myself going somewhere I didn't want to go—as in truth happened often enough later on—because there is some excitement just in moving along.

Besides, the more I thought about it, the more I wanted my name to be in the history books, which for a teacher is after all not so surprising, is it? It isn't all that easy for a woman, you know, if she isn't born a princess or beautiful like Cleopatra. What could a woman do? When you stopped to think about it, there was precious little a woman could do to get her name in the history books.

"But riding a barrel through the Niagara rapids?"

Poor old Miss Fahrquardt. I can just hear what she would

say. No, no, I certainly did not believe as I set out for Niagara
Falls that riding through the rapids in a barrel was a very significant or important thing to do. It was not like inventing the
telegraph or winning a war or being president or making a lot
of money or almost anything else that men do. But it was
something. It was something difficult and dangerous that a
woman could do as well as a man. Women have to start somewhere. They have to do what they can.

"Like smoking cigars?"

Dear Miss Fahrquardt. As much as she changed my life, I
don't think she would have understood. It always amused Mr.
Gravelet so much, my smoking cigars. *Of course* smoking cigars. Why shouldn't women smoke cigars? They have mouths
and tongues and lungs just like men do, and if it is satisfying to
a man, why not to a woman too? Maybe more so, as far as that
goes, like loving. I'm glad to see that some women these days
smoke cigarettes in public places, but you just think about it,
why not cigars? It will be a cold day down below before people
won't look twice at a woman smoking a cigar. I mean a lady.

It was the weather. I've thought about it, I really have—why
I left my home and place of security. The weather in Nebraska
is pretty mean, hot and dry in the summer, cold and hard in
the winter, the wind blowing year-round. You might think
Niagara Falls is no improvement, all that snow, which in fact
I didn't even know about at the time I left Superior.

It was the monotony in Nebraska, everything flattened out
so thin and so much the same that there was nothing to hold
me there. Like I was a tumbleweed and there was not a rock or
stick anywhere to catch and keep me from rolling right over
the edge of the horizon.

Nebraska is not kind. In the summer the sun blazes down
white hot, the dust is always in your eyes and throat, and

sometimes you can hardly breathe. And the wind! Then the winter comes with snow and cold, like Siberia, and the wind never lets up. Wheat grows in the summer if you're lucky, and range cattle survive the winter if you're lucky. It's not an easy life.

But you know, I remember one evening, it was sometime in early September, getting on to fall, which in Nebraska usually is that one day it's hot summer and the next day it's cold winter. But anyway, this one day in September, the world was wonderful. We all noticed it. Matthew came home from his office early and we took a walk. I carried Teddy, who was just a baby, and held Jane, who was three, by one hand, Matthew held Jane's other hand, and we walked down to the creek and watched the sun set through the cottonwoods. The air was so sweet, there wasn't any wind, oh, I don't know, everything seemed to be all right. It was . . . it was as though God were kind.

That was one day in my life in Nebraska.

When I stood looking at Matthew's grave for the last time, the sun was blistering, the sky was yellow, and a fine dust on the wind hurt my eyes and powdered my clothes. There were dust devils rising in surrounding fields.

"Good-bye Matthew," I said, and turned and left.

So I went to Niagara Falls. It was another corner to turn. I've turned three corners in my life. The first was when Miss Fahrquardt set me straight on the road to be a teacher. The second was when I left Nebraska, and the third was when what I did at Niagara Falls was over and done with. Well, we all know what's around the next one. It'll come sooner than later now, I reckon, but I don't worry about it much. Not after what I've been through. Why, I've already faced off death more times than you can shake a stick at, and I'll be ready when it comes.

Mr. Calicutt met me at the train in Niagara Falls. He was a real little fellow, about half my size, and a smarty-pants the like of which I'd seldom seen, and I'd seen plenty. He shook my hand and made as if to take my bags, but I already had them secure, one in each hand, and I doubt if he could have lifted either one of them.

"Welcome to wonderful Niagara Falls!" he said. "I'm Harry Calicutt and I'm the mayor here."

"Do tell," I said in my sharpest voice before I could catch myself. I blushed bright red, for right then I saw myself as he saw me, a bossy schoolmarm still lording it over grown men and women who had been her students. No wonder they weren't all that unhappy in Superior to see me go!

I dropped my suitcases, put my hand gently on Mr. Calicutt's arm, and said, "I'm mighty pleased to meet you, Mr. Calicutt, and I'm so glad to be here." I looked around, helpless like, and said, "You don't suppose we can get someone to help with my bags, do you? I'm all tuckered out."

It was an outright lie, but I'd been telling the truth for years as a teacher, and where had it gotten me?

Mrs. Taylor," he said in that super-concerned fake way of his, "why, of course. "He whistled for a porter, and soon we were in Mr. Calicutt's buggy on the way to a rooming house he had picked out for me.

"You'll want to rest," he said, putting his little hand on my big knee.

"Maybe," I said, looking around. It was just beautiful. It was in the height of summer, and in Nebraska that meant that everything was brown and dead and dry. Here the leaves of all the trees were shining green, everything was green everywhere, the sun was pleasant, and there was just a bit of a nice breeze. "Why, it's just *beautiful* here," I turned to Mr. Calicutt.

He simpered and preened and took credit for the pleasant streets, the nice houses, the big trees, the bright green lawns, and the weather.

"I'll bet you had something to do with the Falls being here, too," I said.

"No, no," he laughed, not too amused. "Mother Nature saw to that. But I was born here next to them, and I'll have to admit that was pretty clever of me."

"Let me get settled down," I said. It was only midmorning. "If you can come back this afternoon we can get down to business. I presume you'd like to get things settled, the contract and all, as soon as possible."

"What? Oh, yes," he said, and went off, looking back at me puzzled. I waved cheerily to him.

I didn't like the looks of the rooming house at all, so I just set my bags down in the room and said to the woman who ran the place, "I've been cooped up in that train for three days and I just have to go for a walk."

She took me out on the porch and pointed where I could go see some nice big houses that had just been built, including the mayor's. I thanked her and moseyed off in the direction she said, but after the first block I turned and walked down toward the river and the railway station. She hadn't pointed that way and I could see that it was the poorer part of town. I patted the flat package in my garter belt—the money I'd got from my sale—and started doing some systematic walking. After about an hour I found what I wanted: a small white house on a shabby street. But the women peeking out at me from the windows of the other houses looked respectable, and there were trees.

"FOR SALE" the sign said. "HARRY CALICUTT, REALTOR."

Good enough, I thought. I walked back up to Main Street

and had a good dinner in the Niagara Falls Cafe. Then I took
in the better part of town, looked at Mayor Calicutt's big new
house, and went by the school. It was a consolidated school,
with all grades through high school, and lots of rooms. School
wouldn't start until fall, but they were cleaning up the play-
ground and doing some painting. I walked by slowly.

I didn't go see the Falls on the river. There'd be time
enough for that.

I asked the landlady at the rooming house if we couldn't
have the parlor for a private meeting, and when Mr. Calicutt
came back I sat him right down at the table with two chairs
pulled up to it. "Here are my railway ticket stubs and the receipts for my traveling expenses," I said, and I spread them out
in front of him.

He looked up at me horrified, and said, "What . . . ?"

"We can take care of that later," I said. "Now just what is it
you want to hire me to do?"

Mr. Calicutt got a grim look on his face, but he did settle
down to business. And it was the most amazing thing! He
didn't want me to ride through the rapids in a barrel at all.
Instead, he started talking about a Mr. Gravelet, a Frenchman, who was a tightrope walker, who had walked on a rope
right across Niagara Falls. Mr. Calicutt had a real proprietary
way of talking about him.

"Wait a minute," I said. "Let me get this straight. Am I to
understand that Mr. Gravelet is in your employ?"

"Why, yes, in a manner of speaking. I'm his manager."

"And . . . ?"

"And what?" Mr. Calicutt asked me.

"Mr. Calicutt," I said, "just what does all this have to do
with me?"

He was pretty flustered and his face got red, but he went

right into it at last. "You see, Mrs. Taylor, Gravelet walks across the river several times each week, and he needs to keep doing new things to attract crowds. He's walked backward and blindfolded and on stilts and he rides a bicycle. But you know how people are—they always want something new. Now in Europe, he used to push people across the rope in a wheelbarrow."

"Stop right there," I said. "Are you saying you want me to ride in a wheelbarrow on a rope across Niagara Falls?"

"Well, I thought . . ."

I pushed back my chair and stood up. "Mr. Calicutt," I said, "how much do you reckon I weigh?"

He looked embarrassed, but I repeated my question. "How much? Don't be polite now, I know how much I weigh. What do you think?"

"One hundred and fifty?" he said in a wee voice.

I guffawed. "Mr. Calicutt! If you were one of my students I'd have to slap you for impertinence. I am a *big* woman. I am five feet seven inches tall, and there have been times when I would have tipped the scales in my birthday suit at 200 pounds. I grant you I don't weigh that much now, but really, Mr. Calicutt, 150 is a dishonest guess." I sat down.

"But dear Mrs. Taylor," he began.

"Dear Mr. Calicutt," I said, "I came here to work for you, and if we're going to do business together, we ought to at least try to start out being honest with each other."

Mr. Calicutt took out his handkerchief and mopped his brow, though it wasn't a hot day. He looked at me, embarrassed, and I smiled at him. Then he laughed nervously, and I joined in, and pretty soon we had a real big laugh together and then he had to wipe his eyes with his handkerchief.

"You are a card, Mrs. Taylor," he said, "a real card."

"Do you really think he could do it?" I asked.

Mr. Calicutt sobered right up. "Absolutely! The man can do anything on that rope. He's a genius. He's more than a genius, he's the greatest tightrope walker that ever lived. He's as safe on that rope as you and I are walking down Main Street. I swear to you, Mrs. Taylor, I would trust my life to him."

"Then why don't you ride in his wheelbarrow?" I asked.

Mr. Calicutt turned green.

"You don't weigh 120 pounds," I said, squinting up my eyes and looking at him. "I'll bet you don't weigh more than 115. You'd be a lot easier to push across than me."

"I really couldn't do it because of my position," he said primly. "The Mayor of Niagara Falls . . . And besides, I'm not a performer."

"I guess I am," I said, laughing to reassure him. "Most teachers are."

"Yes," he said. "That's what I want you to do. Ride across Niagara Falls in a wheelbarrow."

"Will it get my name in the history books?" I asked.

"What?"

"How much do you propose to pay for this performance?"

"Well, now, that depends, Mrs. Taylor, on just how many people come. And how many times you do it. I hadn't thought we'd settle that until we saw how it went."

"You didn't, did you?" I said. I took out a paper I'd prepared. I hadn't been married to a lawyer for nothing.

"I fixed this contract up," I said, "for riding a barrel through the rapids, but it can serve. All we have to do is change the part about riding the rapids to riding a wheelbarrow."

He didn't want to look at the paper, so I went on. "What it says is that I get one hundred dollars the first time and fifty dollars for each repeat."

"One hundred dollars!" Mr. Calicutt said, and this time he stood up. But I just sat there with my arms crossed, leaning on the table, looking up at him, and he sat back down.

"*Mrs. Taylor,*" he said. He laughed in a false way. "Really, Mrs. Taylor."

"That *is* my name," I said.

"It's too much," he said abruptly.

"Then why don't you do it yourself?" I said, picking the paper up.

He took the paper and read it over carefully, making marks on it with a pencil. He thought a while, stuck the pencil lead in his teeth (it was all I could do to keep from whopping it right out of his hand), and then said, "Forty dollars for the first time and twenty for each repeat."

"One hundred," I said. "And fifty."

"Mrs. Taylor," he said, trying to make his voice very cold. "Fifty and twenty-five is absolutely the most that I will give you, and that's my last offer. I am not accustomed to bargaining," he said huffily.

I picked the paper up and folded it and put it back in my bag.

"Let's think on that a while," I said.

I just sat there quiet. I was having so much fun! It never occurred to me that being a schoolteacher was such good preparation for doing business. I just let Mr. Calicutt wiggle.

"Mr. Calicutt," I said, finally, "I wonder if you know of any houses for sale in town?"

That brought him back to life, like a rat terrier smelling a mouse in a corncrib.

"Are you interested in buying a house, Mrs. Taylor?" he asked.

"I don't know," I said, looking around. "The fact is, Mr.

Calicutt," I leaned over the table and spoke confidentially, "I've always lived in a house of my own, and I don't know if I want to live in a rooming house. You know what I mean?"

"Indeed I do, Mrs. Taylor" he said. He closed his hands up into half fists and thumped the table. "Yes," he said, "I know of some houses for sale in town. Why don't we take my buggy and look around?"

"I'd love to go for a ride, Mr. Calicutt," I said.

I let him show me one big house, but when he was done I said, "Mr. Calicutt, I'm a widow. Just a lone woman, and besides that, I don't have the money for such a magnificent house as this one."

"No? Well, I didn't want to underestimate your wealth the way I did your weight," he said.

"You'd better guess again," I said, raising my eyebrows the way my mother used to.

The third house he showed me was the little white one I had in mind. "It's all right," I said, "but don't you have anything cheaper."

That didn't make him happy, and he showed me two more houses about the same price.

"That's it, I'm afraid," he said when he saw I was losing interest. He wasn't pleased with how it was going.

"These last two houses aren't on very nice streets," I said.

"No," he said, trying to figure out where my mind was. He would catch on. "Let's go back to that little white house on Elm Street," he said thoughtfully. "I think you liked that one."

We drove over and sat in the buggy looking at it.

"I'd like it," I said frankly, "but I can't afford it."

This time we talked in his office. "If you'd tell me how much you could put down, Mrs. Taylor, I'm sure we could work out some system of payment by the month for the rest."

I made as though I weren't listening and got out my railway ticket stubs, my receipts, and the contract I'd made out, and put them on the table.

"What is this?" he said, fluttering his hands.

"This is my capital," I said, "plus my willingness to be pushed in a wheelbarrow on a tightrope across Niagara Falls, one hundred dollars the first time and fifty dollars each repeat."

Mr. Calicutt reached out and tapped the contract with his finger.

"You're a hard woman, Mrs. Taylor."

"Some have said so," I agreed.

He didn't laugh.

We dickered for about an hour, and in the end I gave him half of what I'd got from my sale, and the rest of the payments were to be covered by what he owed me for expenses and for my performances.

To tell the truth, I'd never even seen a man walk a tightrope, let alone push someone across in a wheelbarrow. But if this Mr. Gravelet had done it with other folks, he could do it with me. I was just sorry I wouldn't be the first.

I slept in the rooming house that night, but the next day I moved into my little house. Neighbor ladies came over, and pretty soon I had an old bed somebody didn't need and a kitchen table with three chairs and some other odds and ends. That afternoon a woman took me to a place where I bought some more used furniture and some dishes and pans, and I was settled in before you knew it. Mr. Calicutt dropped by to remind me that he'd pick me up tomorrow at one o'clock, to get ready for the wheelbarrow ride that was scheduled for four o'clock. He had a woman along to take my measurements for a costume.

"No sir!" I said the next day when Mr. Calicutt took that suit from a package and spread it out on my new used dining room table. "I will not wear bloomers in a public place."

"They're not bloomers," he said, heated up but trying to be patient. "It's a performer's costume."

"It sure is some costume," I said, "something a dance hall tart might wear, but not a respectable married woman, and a widow besides."

"*Mrs. Taylor*," the little pipsqueak wheedled, "this is the very latest design for lady rope walkers from Paris. It is the *expected* thing to wear."

"Mr. Calicutt," I said, "maybe you have noticed that I'm pretty big in front?"

He blushed, the silly little man.

I went right on. "And truth to tell, I'm pretty big behind too. Really, Mr. Calicutt, do you expect me to get out in front of a lot of people in a suit of underclothes?"

"It's not a suit of underclothes," he said. "It's more like a bathing suit."

"A bathing suit?" I said, taking it from him and holding it up to myself. "Is it maybe your intention that Mr. Gravelet tip me off into the river for a swim?"

I did like the way he turned green. He'd been asked to ride in the wheelbarrow himself, I could tell that, but he was yellow through and through and scared to death to do it. If I hadn't already decided, that would have done it, because I wanted to show that little popinjay that I was just as good and better than he.

I took the suit into the bedroom and put it on. You'd think I was going to a party masquerading as a balloon. "Mr. Calicutt," I yelled through the door.

"Yes, Mrs. Taylor?"

"You don't expect me to go riding through the streets in this outfit, do you?"

"Don't you have anything to put over it?"

"No," I said. I did have a winter coat, but I'd sweat like a pig if I wore it on a summer day.

"You can wrap a blanket around you."

"I am not an Indian squaw, Mr. Calicutt," I replied.

"Damn!" he said. "All right, all right. You just wait here. Don't take off your costume. I'll be right back with something."

He went off, and while he was gone I sat in the front room and smoked a cigar to calm my nerves. What would the neighbor ladies have thought then, if they'd looked in to see me sitting in a pair of white bloomers with red and blue bows stuck all over, looking like nothing more than a clown in a circus? And smoking a cigar.

Mr. Calicutt's eyes nearly popped out of his head when he came back and saw me sitting there, my arms and legs crossed, with that half-smoked cigar sticking out of my mouth. But he didn't say a word about it.

"I have a fine cape for you, Mrs. Taylor," he said, shaking it out so I could see.

I carefully put out my cigar and lay it on the plate I'd been using as an ashtray, and then took the cape. "It's very nice," I said to Mr. Calicutt, and it was. It was a light green velvet with an orange satin lining. I put it on and it covered me quite nicely.

"I got it over at the school," Mr. Calicutt said. "Them's our school colors, and I remembered that the marshal for the band parade wore that cape last year."

"Aren't we ready to go, then?" I said, and I let Mr. Calicutt take my arm and guide me out to his buggy.

I'd never seen so many people. They lined the banks on both sides of the gorge, well down from the Falls, which I got a good look at for the first time. It was an impressive sight, and I particularly liked the seagulls floating in and out of the spray above the foam at the base of the Falls.

And there was Mr. Gravelet, out on that rope over the river. He stood on his head and took big jumps and ran and hopped, and I must say I was relieved to see how he cavorted. Because it sure looked to me that if anybody could push a wheelbarrow across that tightrope, it would be Mr. Gravelet.

Then he came back to the platform and Mr. Calicutt took me up to be introduced.

The two of them glared at each other. Mr. Gravelet was very angry and I could see that Mr. Calicutt was working himself up to be. I stood back and tried not to grin, which wasn't easy, because Mr. Calicutt looked like nothing more than a banty rooster, and Mr. Gravelet . . . Well, if *my* outfit was something, I could hardly believe what that Frenchman was wearing. He had on pink satin tights, pink, mind you, and I mean tight, tight on his body, and I mean everywhere. I had to turn my head to keep from staring. And he had a little short cape halfway down his back, made of green velvet with gold epaulets on his shoulders, and stitched designs all around. He was a tall man, nearly six feet, and he bent over Mr. Calicutt and waved his arms. Tall, but he wasn't a big man, he was thin as could be, though you could see his muscles moving under his tights.

"You are not prepared to ride yourself as you promised," Mr. Gravelet stated. He spoke English right out, not always grammatical, and through his nose like Frenchmen do, but he had no trouble making himself understood.

"I want you to meet Mrs. Taylor," Mr. Calicutt began.

"She's too big," Mr. Gravelet snapped, not even looking at me.

"People are watching," Mr. Calicutt hissed.

And you know, an amazing thing happened. Mr. Gravelet slowly straightened up, he relaxed, the way you see a cat or a dog do when it lies down. I'd never seen a human being do that before. The lines left his face, his anger was gone, and he turned to me smiling. "You're perfectly right," he said to Mr. Calicutt though he was looking at me. "Thank you for reminding me."

He took me by the hand. "And you, dear lady, I am pleased to make your acquaintance."

That's what he said, and I said, "I'm mighty pleased to meet you too, Mr. Gravelet."

"Everything will be perfectly all right, you are not to worry at all," he said. Then he lifted my hand in his, his arm curved, and he gracefully turned us around like we were in a dance in a play, and we walked up onto that platform where the rope was tied. He unfastened my cape and pulled it off so it swirled out flat in a big arc in the air, and then he bent down and kissed my hand.

My mouth fell open and I just looked at him. I totally forgot about my costume and all those people watching us. Why I'd have ridden in that man's wheelbarrow stark naked.

Nevertheless, I was plenty nervous. He calmed me and talked to me and patted me on the shoulder as he helped me get in the wheelbarrow. He was so confident I almost forgot to be scared. Anyway, I knew I had to pretend not to be, I could see Mr. Gravelet expected that of me. So I tried to relax and before I knew it there we were, out in the most empty and open space I'd ever been in in all my life, going right over that river on that rope. I tell you, I was so scared!

"Keep your eyes open," Mr. Gravelet said gently. "You have to see to keep your balance. Look straight back along the rope." I was facing him. "Don't look down. Just relax, you're doing wonderfully."

He spoke to me real encouraging all the way across, but I was terrified and couldn't say a word.

Before you knew it, we were across and people were cheering. Mr. Gravelet helped me out of the wheelbarrow in such a wonderfully graceful way, and stood there with his elbow out and holding my arm up to show me off.

Well, I took to it, that I did. I might have been a big woman, but I knew about posture and how to stand—I'd been teaching it long enough. I smiled and waved and the crowd cheered. Then I turned and held my hand out and bent toward Mr. Gravelet so they would see I thought he was the hero. He was pleased at that, and took a bow.

We stood and talked to people, and I signed autographs for the first time in my life. That was really something. Then Mr. Gravelet said to me, "They'd like us to go back. It would be good for the show."

The thought chilled me to the bone. I looked across to the other side and it looked miles. But I just nodded and let him help me in the wheelbarrow again. The second time was worse, and I couldn't help but look down a few times, a long, long way down. My bowels were was so cramped up that I didn't have a movement for three days after.

But it was all right. And I didn't have time to dwell on the thought of having to do it again, because I had to argue with Mr. Calicutt about whether a performance was one-way or a round trip. I won because Mr. Gravelet said it was one-way. He laughed kind of funny when he said it, and Mr. Calicutt turned green again, and gave in.

The next time I felt perfectly comfortable. I got to looking around and began to enjoy it. I knew I was safe as could be with Mr. Gravelet. And I did enjoy the applause and the crowds and signing my autograph.

Can you believe it, after a dozen times it got almost boring. That happens when you do anything over and over again. I noticed that teaching school.

"I feel like a tub of lard," I said to Mr. Gravelet one day, "being pushed across in that wheelbarrow. Isn't there something more I can do?" I was hoping he would teach me to walk the tightrope. No woman had ever done that, or at least not across the Niagara. I knew there were lots of women tightrope walkers in Europe. I'd seen pictures of them in Mr. Gravelet's scrapbook.

"I don't know," Mr. Gravelet said. But he thought about it, and he said, "Did you ever stand on your head?"

"Did I?" I laughed. "When I was seven years old I won the standing-on-your-head contest for the entire school of Hardy, Nebraska." Mr. Gravelet looked puzzled, so I said, "We all stood on our heads at the same time and the one who stayed up the longest won."

"Oh," he said. Then he proceeded to teach me how to stand on my head in the wheelbarrow, first on the ground, and then on a practice rope.

"Very good! Mrs. Taylor," which made me laugh the way he said it, "*Très bien!*" in French, so I'd almost lose my balance. But I *was* very good.

It was Mr. Hurd who had those contests, but now I thought what Miss Fahrquardt would think, me some forty years later standing on my head in a wheelbarrow on a tightrope 200 feet above the water at Niagara Falls. Goodness knows what she would have said, but I do know it was a spectacular sight. And

I was the first and only person ever to do it, or to ride across in a wheelbarrow for that matter, let alone stand on my head. But that's not why my name is in the history books. I'll come to that later.

One time as a practical joke Mr. Calicutt hid the wheelbarrow. Mr. Gravelet was frantic, and I could see the tendons standing out as he clenched his jaw.

"He knows I've done this in Europe," Mr. Gravelet said. "But she was just a child."

I didn't know what he was talking about, but I soon found out.

He breathed out heavy and his shoulders dropped as he turned to me and said, "Do you think you could ride across on my back?"

"I'm too big," I said at once.

"You are big," he said seriously, "but I am strong."

"Do you *really* think you can, Mr. Gravelet?" I asked.

"I can," he said.

I wanted to tell him he shouldn't try it, but I knew he had to. I'd seen little boys like that all my life, faced with something too big for them that they had to do. Often they managed to do it, one way or another.

Mr. Gravelet looked to me to be a man of about thirty-five. He swore he was thirty, but I never believed him. He was about six feet tall as I said, but he couldn't have weighed more than 140 pounds. Skin and bones. And muscle.

I slipped off my shoes. He turned around and I got on his back. He stepped out on the tightrope and we were on our way.

Sweat broke out on Mr. Gravelet in streams, and my whole front against his back was wet. We went on slower and slower and about halfway I said, "Stop."

Mr. Gravelet stopped.

"You're getting too tired," I said. "You're going to have to rest."

"Yes," he said.

I slid off and there I was standing on the tightrope! That was a thrill, I tell you, and that rope sure felt good through my stocking feet. And big. "Mr. Gravelet," I said, "why don't I just walk along behind you like this the rest of the way? I'm sure I can do it."

He stiffened. "Get on my back, Mrs. Taylor," he said. And I did.

That second half was uphill and it was a lot more work for him than the first, but I could tell he was so determined that nothing would stop him. When he set out to do something, nothing could ever stop him. That was the kind of man Mr. Gravelet was, and that was why he was so great.

I asked him several times if he would teach me to walk the tightrope. I knew I could do it. "I walked along the tops of wooden fences when I was a girl," I said to him.

"It's not the same," he said.

Mr. Gravelet was almost never gruff to me, but he wouldn't teach me to walk the tightrope. I figured he knew quite well that I could learn, but he wouldn't teach me because he didn't want any competition.

I always regretted not learning to walk the tightrope, because if I had, things might have gone different for me than they did, But Mr. Gravelet wouldn't teach me, and that was that.

Mr. Gravelet and I actually got on real well. He was kind of lost in America even if his English, which he learned in England, was good for a foreigner. I helped him improve it, except there was nothing anybody could do for his accent. I thought it was sweet, but it sounded affected and effeminate to most people, which made a lot of men dislike Mr. Gravelet who might otherwise have found cause to be his friend if he hadn't talked so through his nose. He did have such a big nose! It made children laugh.

But if he wouldn't teach me to walk the tightrope, he did pay more attention to me. "We should be seen in public together, Mrs. Taylor," he said. "It's good for business."

So we went out to restaurants to eat together. Oh, we were quite the celebrities. I caught right on to it, like I'd always been giving folks my autograph, and pretending people weren't watching and talking about us when they were.

And if I had to wear that dumb outfit—I don't care if lady rope walkers in Europe wore them, those bloomers would look silly on any woman big as I was—I sure made up for it with other clothes. For I'll say one thing about Mr. Gravelet, he was a Frenchman and knew about clothes. We went to Buffalo and New York City and I bought a wardrobe you wouldn't believe. Really, I believe I was the best-dressed woman in all of New York State.

Mr. Gravelet was a dresser himself, with a black beret on his head and one of those colored scarves Frenchmen wear around their necks. But when it was formal he wore a big flowing tie, a short coat, and tight trousers. Those trousers. I had to keep from looking at him, but other women looked, you'd better believe.

Anyway, we were like actors on a stage, and it behooved us to be bigger and even better than real life. Folks looked up to us, and we were in the business of entertaining them.

Those were the good days and I rode across Niagara Gorge on a tightrope in Mr. Gravelet's wheelbarrow twenty-eight times that summer, and once on his back. Every time was a thrill and after the first two times I was never afraid. Twenty-nine times taken across, and that's a record that's never been broken, but it wasn't why I'd come to Niagara Falls. And as the time came closer for Mr. Gravelet to return to France, because he'd never intended to settle in America despite his great successes here, Mr. Calicutt reminded me of what I'd come for.

"You mean you still want me to ride the rapids in a barrel?" I asked.

"How will you pay off what you still owe on the house otherwise?" he said.

I'd forgotten all about it, but now I was going to ride the rapids in a barrel after all. So the summer had been just an interlude, all the time the river waiting to take me. And strange to say, it was harder for me now than it would have been before, because riding the rapids in a barrel wasn't going to be so very nice as in Mr. Gravelet's wheelbarrow.

Mr. Calicutt took me to a cooper so I could see how I fit in the barrel. It looked solid enough. Of course it was uncomfortable when I got inside, but what could you expect?

The cooper pounded on the outside of the barrel with the flat of his hand and said, "Don't you worry, you'll be safe as a bug in a rug going over the Falls in this barrel."

I let them help me out of the barrel and I stood looking at it a moment, and then I turned to Mr. Calicutt and said, "*Over the Falls?*"

"Why, yes, Mrs. Taylor," he said, trying to make nothing of it. "People's already gone down the rapids."

"What is this?" Mr. Gravelet said at noon the next day, coming in the kitchen door of my little house without even knocking as he usually did. He had in his hand a poster he had torn off a wall.

"Oh, that," I said glancing at it. "Sit down, I've just about got dinner ready."

"But you can't do this thing," he said. "It's insane, madness, suicide." He sat down and tucked his napkin in his shirt.

"That's what I came here for," I said, sliding a big piece of ham from the skillet onto his plate.

He attacked it the funny way Frenchmen have with the knife and fork in the wrong hands and said, "You did not. You told me you came here to ride a barrel in the rapids, below the Falls."

"It's been done."

"So?" he said.

He leaned back while I put mashed potatoes on his plate and shoved the bowl of gravy toward him. I served myself and sat down opposite him. "You can't do something first a second time," I said.

"What?"

"I'll be the first person to go over Niagara Falls in a barrel."

"This ham is good," he said. "I'm getting used to American cooking."

"To *my* cooking," I laughed. "It's me you're getting used to." He blushed just a tiny bit, and I laughed again.

"No," he said. "It's crazy. That's why nobody's done it."

"Have you seen the barrel?" I asked him.

"The barrel? You mean that idiot manager of ours has already had a barrel made? What does he know about making barrels? Is he an engineer?"

Mr. Gravelet ate the rhubarb pie I had prepared for dessert. "This is very good," he said, and went right on with his mouth full. "Where," he asked, "where is this wonderful barrel that will carry a person safely over Niagara Falls?"

"Come along, I'll show you," I said.

Mr. Gravelet fumed as we walked to the cooper's. It wasn't very far from my house. He looked at the barrel, and then turned to the cooper who was telling him how strong it was and said, "Give me that mallet."

The cooper wasn't eager to do it, so Mr. Gravelet took the mallet out of his hand and started pounding all around the barrel. Before you knew it, one of the staves had sprung.

"So much for your barrel," Mr. Gravelet said, tossing the mallet down.

The cooper was furious, but Mr. Gravelet pushed him aside and walked over to his work table. "Get me a large piece of paper and some pencils," he said.

"Yes, do," I said to the cooper, holding him firmly by the arm. "Mr. Gravelet is an engineer."

"I do not approve," Mr. Gravelet said, "but if you are going to do this thing, you must have a proper barrel."

The cooper never liked Mr. Gravelet, but he built a new barrel to his design. And it saved my life.

The next day Mr. Gravelet tried to talk Mr. Calicutt into having me ride the barrel through the rapids below the Falls instead of going over it. I was quite angry with him about this. "There is no point in my riding a barrel through the rapids below the Falls, Mr. Gravelet," I told him.

"It makes a good show, I'm told," he said.

"You don't understand," I said to him. I was quite heated up. "It's already been done."

He bowed his head slightly.

"A man has already done it first," I said.

He smiled.

"A woman can do anything a man can do, Mr. Gravelet," I said firmly. I was still vexed that he would not teach me to walk the tightrope.

He bowed again and lowered his eyelids. He always treated women right, but he did not think highly of their abilities. Oh, he liked them for what they could do. He did that! But he sure thought they had their place. "Beneath men," he'd say, trying to get a rise out of me.

I was right to want to go over Niagara Falls in a barrel. You might say that I already had a place in history by riding in Mr. Gravelet's wheelbarrow, and maybe I did. But if so, it was a mighty small place. I saw in an encyclopedia where it says that Mr. Gravelet carried people across Niagara Falls in his wheelbarrow. *People,* no mention of me or my name nor that I was the first and only one. So I was right to think that brave as I might have been in doing it, and even standing on my head, riding across the tightrope in Mr. Gravelet's wheelbarrow isn't worth a hill of beans to history. It had to be better than that.

The first person to go over Niagara Falls on purpose and survive alive, man or woman—that's what it had to be. And how much more spectacular and significant that it be a woman, and that woman be me, Anna Edson Taylor, a name henceforth that could not be reduced merely to *people* and left out of history books. Because when they come to firsts in history, there could be only one and she'd have to be named and that name would be me.

Anna Edson Taylor. I planned to be the first person to go over Niagara Falls, voluntarily, on purpose, in a barrel, to live and tell her story.

The important part was to tell the story, because lecturing on what I'd done was how I planned to put some money aside for my old age. I'd already made up my speech.

Over Niagara Falls in a barrel! "Miss Fahrquardt," I would have said, "you taught me that we're all set here on this earth for a purpose. I have been fortunate enough to find mine."

If I came to Niagara Falls not knowing it would be over the Falls and not just down the rapids, I didn't know I'd be riding in Mr. Gravelet's wheelbarrow on the tightrope either, but I took to that right nicely and it was a good thing. Now it would be in the barrel over the Falls, and that was just fine with me.

October 4th was the day set for my ride. Mr. Gravelet's boat to Europe sailed on October 10th, and as his tightrope had been taken down and he was without anything to do, I said to him, "Mr. Gravelet, why don't you and I go to New York City to see the sights? You can help me shop for my wardrobe for my lecture tour."

"That's a splendid idea," he said. He liked to use those elegant words.

He got us nice rooms in a good hotel and every evening we went out to a fine restaurant. I spent every last penny I had left on clothes. Mr. Gravelet wanted to buy me some clothes too, but I wouldn't let him, except for one pretty scarf because he so wanted to get me a present to remember him by.

When we walked about, people knew who we were. I'm sure those days on the avenues increased by thousands the number of people who came to see me go over the Falls. They even had to put on special trains to transport folks.

I hesitate now what to say about Mr. Gravelet and me. He was a most elegant man. Not handsome, really, but striking, someone people turned to look at because of the way he held his head and moved his body and wore his clothes and looked around, like he was glad to be in the world and knew the world was improved by his presence. He brought that out in me too, and big as I was, with a round face plain as mud, I was always something else when I was with Mr. Gravelet. He treated me like a lady, and I acted like one. Nobody was fooled. People knew we weren't rich or royalty. But, oh, how we preened!

Mr. Gravelet. He was a man, like other men. And I was a woman. Men always want a woman for what men want a woman for, and big and ugly as I was there were always men who wanted me for that. Mr. Gravelet did.

"I need you, Annie," he said, and who was I to say no? Didn't I want to cuddle him, too? And hold him tight?

"I love you, Annie," he said. "*Je t'aime.*"

I believed him. For the moment, anyway, why not? *Pourquoi-pas?* Because I was soft on him and it did no harm and he was a ma n I could admire and respect. He was a real artist and devoted to his work and he certainly showed that he cared for me. He was younger than me by quite a few years, but I always was a motherly woman. When he was sad as men sometimes are, I held his head on my breast.

"My father sold me to a circus when I was five years old," he told me once.

"There, there," I said, holding him tight.

"They locked me in a cage to keep me from running away."

He was a little boy and I was his mama. Sometimes in the night he whimpered and I held him to protect him from his fears.

"I know exactly how I shall die too," he said when I told him about Matthew dying of TB.

That always gave me the chills. For though he was a brave man and knew his trade and I felt perfectly safe on the tight-rope in his wheelbarrow, he had to do it all his life. And he knew that one day he would fall. Who could deny it? That can't be a good thing for a man to have running in his head, always knowing someday there would be a false step that would take him to his doom.

"It's a comfort to know, Annie," he said. "Really it is. Most men don't think of death. They don't know how they're going to die. They even pretend they won't die. I know it every minute of my life, and exactly how it will come."

I held him and loved him. Men don't need much for comfort, but they need it bad! So bad it's funny. But it's a very serious thing with them, and I always watched not to laugh. Men are so unsure with a woman that you can wilt them down with just a sideways glance, so I was always careful to keep up their pride and let them know how good they were and how pleased I was.

I really liked being loved, but I liked almost as much holding a man and being held and loved for what I could give him. And truth to tell, as often as not it's a good thing that was enough for me, but of course you could never let them know. Matthew never thought to notice what I was feeling, but Mr. Gravelet set some store on his way with a woman and he watched me close. So I always let him know I was gratified whether it really came to me or not, which didn't matter because just loving and doing for him was enough. I knew nothing could ever come from it, me an older woman and all, but I wish . . .

Oh, I wish he'd taught me how to walk the tightrope. It vexes me still. I mean, what good is it to be able to stand on your head if you don't even know how to walk?

People knew, of course. People always know. Mr. Gravelet came to my house, and I didn't do anything special to try to conceal it. It put me on bad terms with some of the neighbor ladies who had been such help to me when I moved in, but they'd already grown cool when they found out what my work was. But a lot of what people said about Mr. Gravelet and me just wasn't true. I paid no mind to slander because what did they know?

"It's good for business," Mr. Calicutt said, trying to get my goat by pretending to be scandalized at what someone had said about Mr. Gravelet and me, which I wouldn't have known if he hadn't told me. "It is shocking, Mrs. Taylor, the stories some people will tell."

"That it is," I'd say, looking right at him.

But I knew that even there Mr. Calicutt was right. It was part of the show, people thinking those wild things about Mr. Gravelet and me. And the ounce of truth in it, well, I suppose that spiced the loaf.

The day came, as one day after another always does. I got up that morning and poked around cleaning the house. Mr. Gravelet was coming for dinner at noon, and he was going to take me up the river to where the boat with the barrel already was.

It's no good having nothing to do. I sat there in the parlor and it was like I was sick or something. My legs felt weak and I had chills up my spine. It wasn't like being afraid so much as it was just that there wasn't anything more that I could do until this was over. And whatever happened, well, afterward it would be different. I'd never see my little house like this again, it would all be changed. It already seemed strange. If I made it, and I couldn't think anything else, all would be wonderful. If I didn't . . . it wouldn't matter.

I got up and prepared dinner, though I sure didn't want much of anything to eat myself.

"No, you shouldn't eat very much," Mr. Gravelet said firmly. "You'll get shaken up and you might get seasick. Throwing up in that barrel wouldn't be pleasant. No, you just drink some tea and maybe eat a cracker. I, on the other hand," he expanded his chest and sat down in his chair, "I must eat to keep up my strength, because it will be an enormous effort for me on the shore to keep that barrel upright and to see that it floats smoothly down the river in perfect position to go over the Falls."

I knew it was going to be all right whenever Mr. Gravelet was talking to me. He wasn't just pretending either. Mr. Gravelet never pretended. He always knew, with all his soul and body, just how the performance was going to go, and that it would be successful. Once he saw I was determined, he never tried to talk me out of it again.

This time I did wear a bathing suit, the latest model, specially made for me to my measurements in New York City. It was black with lots of white trim, and I wore it out in the open on the boat without any cape.

It all went awfully fast. There were some people to watch me get on the boat, but the crowds were down where the barrel would come over the Falls. Mr. Gravelet was very professional and took care of me. Mr. Calicutt was there, of course, but I can't remember a word he said. It was like Mr. Gravelet and I were in a world all our own. He helped me get in the barrel and seated me properly, saw that the straps I had to hang onto were tight, checked the cushions for my head.

"*Bonne chance, ma chérie!*" he said, "Good luck!" He kissed my hand, and then he squeezed it real hard.

"I'll be all right." I could barely talk, but I said it.

Mr. Gravelet nodded to the men and they put on the lid. All this time the boat was churning across the river. And just as soon as the lid was tight the barrel was hoisted up and dropped into the river and I was on my way.

Afterward, a lot of people asked me what it was like, going over the Falls, and I told them it was like nothing so much as having a baby, which is true, but not the way most of them took it. I wasn't referring to the pain, nor even to the birth of

something new in the world as one nice newspaperwoman put
it. She thought I meant the accomplishment itself as a wonderful and dangerous thing a woman had done, and bringing
something into the world that wasn't there before. That's
true, for now it's a fact that someone has gone over the Falls in
a barrel, and it was me who did it. But what I meant was not
the pain of having it nor the bringing forth of something new,
but just the waiting for it to happen, the endurance and the set
of mind needed not to get hysterical. Just like being pregnant
and waiting to have a baby. You have to persevere.

Because that was what it was like, even before getting in the
barrel. It was that way in New York City, in the restaurants, in
the clothes salons and millineries seeing the sights, and yes,
even in Mr. Gravelet's arms. Even in his bed I was already on
my way down the river above Niagara Falls, holding on, holding out, enduring and surviving, as I knew I must. For like
being pregnant and having a baby, there was no turning back,
and I knew that. It isn't always easy, knowing what must
come. Still, you have to go on living and so I did, while all the
time I could see and hear it looming up in my mind, the mist
and the roar and all that water rolling over to fall down and
down so hard.

I was on my way and had to face it long before I was in that
barrel in the water.

When they dumped me out of the boat, the barrel was
caught in the current and flipped upright. It was almost silent
once the boat was gone, and though I couldn't see, I felt that I
was flying down the river. Then I hit the rapids above the
Falls. I hung on to the straps and tried not to bump my head.
It took me nearly twenty minutes to reach the Falls, they said,
but it seemed no time at all to me.

I could hear the roar coming up fast, and I knew when it

happened. I was facing front and the barrel tipped forward. There was a kind of silence in the roar, and then I was thrust up against the top of the barrel. I can't describe how suddenly there was a force that took the barrel down and down and down like, oh, like a locomotive going straight down into the bowels of hell. I don't know that I thought that then, it was what I made up for my talk, but something like that anyway. It was the moment I had been waiting for, and it would be over very soon and then the outcome of all those months of waiting would be known.

I must have passed out. At least all I ever could recall was going down, down, and then it was over. The barrel was bobbing back and forth, spinning slowly. And I was just there, waiting again.

It seemed a longer time than before, and I could hardly believe that it was over and that was all there was. So when they caught the barrel and tipped it, I got in a panic for fear it really wasn't done and *now* the fall was coming. But it was just the men who pulled the barrel to a rock and took off the top. I felt too weak to move and was too big for them to pull me out.

But when one of them took a sledge and started to smash open the barrel, I came right to my senses. "I can get out, don't hurt my barrel," I said, and with their help I did struggle out. The men held me, but I made my own way from rock to rock until I got to shore.

They said I made no sense and was not right for half a day. That's just poppycock. I was all worked up because they weren't saving my barrel. I stopped and turned around and yelled at them, "Save my barrel!" But they just pulled me on to shore.

"Delirious," one of them said.

"Delirious, my foot!" I said to him. "That barrel's my livelihood. Never you mind about me, I'm all right. Save my barrel!"

But it wasn't until we got down to the boat dock of the *Maid of the Mist* that I could get anybody to pay me any mind. "Mr. Calicutt," I shouted the minute I saw him. "They're busting up my barrel."

He sure knew exactly what I meant because his profit as well as mine was tied up in that barrel. He moved out of there fast with some men to fetch it back.

Mr. Gravelet took me to his hotel, where he had a room prepared with a hot bath. I sure needed it because it was October and I was wet and cold and also bruised all over black and blue. I had never gone to Mr. Gravelet's hotel before, and I knew doing it now would be the source of more scurrilous slanders on my name, but I was too done in to care. After my hot bath I wrapped up in the bedclothes and slept almost a day. But I'd done it. I put my name in the history books.

Then the newspaper men came.

"I've never owned a cat," I told one of them.

"But why did you put your little cat in the barrel, Mrs. Taylor?" he went right on just like he hadn't heard me.

"It wasn't my cat," I said, "and I didn't put it in the barrel."

It was Mr. Calicutt who did it. He saw an opportunity to use the barrel that Mr. Gravelet said was no good, so the week before I was to go over, he sent it off with a cat in it. I never heard of such a thing! The poor little cat. Of course it was dead when they fished the barrel out at the bottom of the Falls. And the newspapers said it was my cat!

"I don't even own a cat," I told the man. "I've never owned a cat."

"Don't you like cats, Mrs. Taylor?" he asked.

"It's not so much I don't like cats," I said, frustrated because

I knew he wouldn't understand. "It's sort of that they don't like me. When I'm around cats my eyes get puffy and I get a runny nose. I get all plugged up if I handle a cat. I can't tolerate them being around if I want to breathe."

It was my own fault. He published in the newspaper that I couldn't tolerate cats, and that I had meanly put my pet cat in that barrel. But if I can't tolerate cats, would I have a pet one? I know that's schoolroom logic and nobody sees the discrepancy. And what could I do when that little traitor, Mr. Calicutt, goes and tells them behind my back that it was my cat? It was a dumb thing for him to do, too, because it might affect people coming to my lectures, of which he got a cut.

The first talk I gave after going over the Falls went just fine. There were over 500 people there, and they were attentive, and the newspapermen were good to me. It was only later that they got vicious.

We hired the Masonic hall and there was a big vase with hothouse flowers in it on the platform where I stood. Mr. Gravelet was there with me—his boat had not yet sailed. And was I dressed pretty! I had a new hat and gown, and oh that hat! They don't wear hats like that today, but it was *big,* and I can hardly describe it. It had feathers and beads and flat bows, and a wide brim all around, and over my eyes there was a veil. The top was dark green velvet that rose up and spilled over each side like on a king's crown. My gown matched, real green silk, smooth and thick. I don't think they get silk like that now, not that thick, with long arms and the skirt billowing on the tops of my shoes. I had new black patent leather shoes, with shiny black bead buttons, and sheer gloves, fawn-colored, and a big brooch made of hundreds of little red garnets pinned on my breast.

I walked out on the stage with Mr. Calicutt and Mr.

Gravelet on either side of me. Mr. Calicutt introduced me, and then they sat down on two chairs and it was up to me. Well, I'd taught children to give speeches all my life, and it would have been a sad thing if I didn't know how to give one myself. I talked right to the audience and I know they liked it. I told them some of the things about my past life, but what they liked most was the dramatic parts of my going over the Falls.

When my talk was done Mr. Gravelet came and stood beside me, tall and elegant, and Mr. Calicutt had gone off the stage and got a big bunch of roses, which he came and gave me. Then he stood off to one side and the audience cheered and it was, really, well, the proudest day of my life.

That was the high point. A few days later I went to New York City with Mr. Gravelet to see him off on his boat back to Europe. Then at my very next talk people weren't attentive and laughed and some of them made rude remarks.

Maybe that first time it was Mr. Gravelet there on the platform that kept them quiet, he was truly an imposing figure of a man. But no, I know they liked me that first time. But without him there they went after me, and Mr. Calicutt, he smirked and wasn't any help at all, though he was losing money and ought to have stood up for me.

I couldn't continue. I couldn't even go over Niagara Falls again because they passed a law against it and Mr. Calicutt wouldn't take the chance of being fined. It was because the newspapers had all written against it. They said I was crazy, and that such a stunt should never have been allowed. This was because Niagara Falls was sacred, Nature's wonder, and ought not to be soiled by the likes of me.

That was so unfair. They never wrote anything like that about Mr. Gravelet and his tightrope. I soon saw what it was.

It was because I was a woman. They didn't like the fact that a woman had been the first to do it. If it had been a man who had gone over Niagara Falls in a barrel for the first time, they'd have praised him to the sky. How *brave* he would have been, how *marvelous* to do it. And they'd probably have even let him do it twice.

It's always that way with men. They stick together. I had shown them what a woman could do and they never allowed that it was any good. They didn't look at what I'd done, the strength I'd had in doing it, the determination. No, they just said it was a crazy stunt. And the woman who'd done it was a lunatic. And a whore—of course they all said that—a crazy whore.

They harped and harped on that one string until they destroyed the wonder and greatness of what I'd done and took away my livelihood and hopes. I couldn't even go back to teaching school once I saw my lecture tour was no good. Everybody knew who I was and nobody was going to hire a crazy woman to teach their children.

I wasn't beat yet, not by a long shot. People were still interested in what I'd done, and nothing could take away from me that I was the first person in the whole wide world to go over Niagara Falls and live to tell the story.

It was my idea to have photographs made up into postcards, so Mr. Calicutt got a nice big selection. There were pictures of me beside the barrel, getting in, going over the Falls, and coming out of the water afterward, and also of Mr. Gravelet on the tightrope. There was one real nice one of me standing on my head in the wheelbarrow out in the middle of the gorge. Mr. Calicutt arranged for a booth beside the Falls and set my barrel there to attract tourists, and I sold postcards and other souvenirs.

There was even a little pamphlet, "The Story of My Life," which I sold. It was all lies. Mr. Calicutt had some newspaper man write it.

"Show business, Mrs. Taylor, show business," Mr. Calicutt said when I complained. I set it in back and sold it only to people who knew about it and asked for it. I don't have a copy anymore, and I'm glad to say there isn't one in the Niagara Falls Public Library. They've got a history collection, and I go there sometimes to read old newspapers about Mr. Gravelet and about me going over the Falls. It's a quiet place, and nice and warm in winter. They know who I am there.

So all my lecture engagements fell through and all my money was gone. I hadn't managed to pay off what I owed on my house, mostly because I spent so much money on clothes, which I don't regret.

It's like Mr. Gravelet once said. He was always checking the guy ropes on his tightrope, and when one looked the least bit frayed he'd throw it away and put in a new one.

"That's a terrible waste, Mr. Gravelet," I said to him.

"No, Mrs. Taylor," he said, "it's not. It's our lives up there, and you should never take chances by cutting corners."

"But you might use that rope some way," I said.

"No," he said, "it never pays. Whenever I set up, I use new ropes. Each place is different and I build for that place. The old ropes are no good. When they've served their purpose, you should get rid of them."

He did like to preach.

"When you go for the main chance, Mrs. Taylor," he said, "you should use the best equipment you can get. And when you're through with it, let it go. Don't look back. And never regret the expenses or losses."

And that's just the way I feel. I went for the main chance and I don't regret it.

I don't hate Mr. Calicutt, though I quit speaking to him after he took my barrel. He got my little house back, too, legal enough, and nothing's fair. He took my barrel to put in a curiosity museum he started, and that was a cruel blow because it was what attracted people to my booth. But I made him give me rights to all the postcards, and I still sell some of them to this day.

We arranged that I could stay in my house, my downpayment on it going as rent. And he gave me some money from that first lecture. It was a hard winter for me, all alone, but the next summer with the booth and selling souvenirs, I got along.

You know Mr. Calicutt was nothing, really, but a conniving grasping skunk, so low a worm that I felt too far above him to despise him. And I couldn't hate the man who had brought me to Niagara Falls, to meet and work with Mr. Gravelet, and to do the thing that put my name forever in the history books.

Every cloud has a silver lining? Oh, poppycock.

After I lost my house I went to California and stayed with my daughter, Jane. She had a lovely home in Carmel, the loveliest place in the world. She married an engineer, you know, and he was the kindest man. And her two daughters were so nice, I doted on them. One was named Annie, after me. They're married now, and I'm a great-grandmother. They had plenty of money and they said, "Grandma, you just sit here at home and take it easy," but I said, "No, for goodness sakes, I'm strong and fit and I don't want to take charity." So I got a job as a clerk in a gift shop, a refined place, I didn't want to embarrass them by taking just any menial job.

And Teddy, too, he was in San Francisco. He did real well in the dry goods business, and he became a manager. Then, you know what? He married the owner's daughter! Now he runs the business and has four big sons. One of his sons he named Matthew, and you know, that boy was sharp as a tack and went on and became a lawyer, just like my Matthew. I was real proud.

They were all good to me, and Jane's husband especially said he wanted me to stay, and Teddy's wife said I could come live with them. But I was restless in California. There isn't any winter there, you know, hardly any change of seasons at all. So I saved up my money and came back to Niagara Falls. It seemed to me that this was where I belonged. My children did want me to stay in California, and that's the truth, but I didn't want to impose on them. I have seen the Pacific Ocean.

And you know what else? One day Mr. Gravelet came back to Niagara Falls and came to my place and bought some postcards.

"Why, Mr. Gravelet!" I said. "How wonderful it is to see you again. How are you?"

"I'm just fine, Mrs. Taylor, and my, it does look as though you're prospering."

"Yes, I am," I said.

And I just wanted to hug him, but I could see he was embarrassed because by then I was an old woman and he was still a man in his prime. After I said I was glad to see him and he said he was glad to see me that was about all we had to say. I actually felt sorry for him, because though they said he'd gotten rich, they also said he'd lost his nerve and didn't walk the tightrope anymore. They wanted him to do it at Niagara Falls again, but he wouldn't. They said that right in the newspaper.

My name is Anna Edson Taylor. My name is in the history books because I am the first person, man or woman, to go over Niagara Falls in a barrel. I am the first person to go over the Falls in any fashion and *live*. For Sam Patch just dived in beside the Falls and Mr. Gravelet just walked on a tightrope over the gorge downstream below the Falls.

I am the one, the first and only one, who truly went over Niagara Falls and survived.

Well, they could say bad things, but they couldn't take away from me what I'd done. It's there in the history books to prove. For I *was* the first and only one, there couldn't be another, the one to go first over Niagara Falls in a barrel and live. But those men were jealous, and though they couldn't take away what I'd done, they did call me a crazy whore and my triumph just a stunt, as though it lacked legitimacy, like I'd born a bastard. And they said a man put me up to it anyway. Let me tell you, it may take a man to get a woman pregnant, but she has to go on and have the baby all by herself.

Mr. Calicutt even suggested I change my name. "Then you could get a job teaching school again," he said.

Change my name? Ha! That's a laugh. Not bloody likely, as Mr. Gravelet used to say.

Don't you forget my name. Anna Edson Taylor. Edson's my maiden name, sometimes they spell it with an "i," Edison, like the inventor, but that's not right. I'm my own person and it's Edson, Anna Edson Taylor.

Remember me, what I did, on October 4th, 1901, Anna Edson Taylor, a widowed schoolteacher, admitted age forty-one, but I was really forty-five. The first person ever to go over

Niagara Falls on purpose, in a barrel, and survive, to live, having done as a woman a dangerous and wondrous thing, as good as any man. I always said forget-me-not was my favorite flower, and I ask you don't forget me now, Anna Edson Taylor, and what I've done.

That's about it. You don't care how I get along now. Not too well, thank you, anymore, but that's the way it goes when you get old. I don't worry about it. I get along.

True, it's not the way I thought it would be. I got my name in the history books, all right, but I'd expected to make some money lecturing to put aside for my old age, and I'd expected people to respect what I did. I sure didn't think they'd turn on me and call me crazy and a whore. But it was mostly men who did that and I don't suppose they could help themselves, seeing as they're weaker than a woman when it comes to holding on and enduring. They lack patience, even Mr. Gravelet didn't have much of that.

Anyway, I showed what a woman could do as good as any man, and I was the first, and my name is in the history books.

ANNA EDSON TAYLOR

I have this dream—and it's not a nightmare though it might sound like one—in which I'm floating down a river. I'm not in a barrel or anything, I'm just there, sort of above the water and going along. Then I come to this big falls and go over.

It's not frightening at all. It's a good feeling. I just float out over the edge and I'm free and happy falling, gently falling.

Colophon

Niagara was designed by Allan Kornblum at Coffee House Press. The Adobe Caslon type and Ponderosa display were outputted at Hi Rez Studio in Grant's Pass, Oregon. This book was printed on acid-free paper and was smyth sewn, to insure longevity and ease of handling.